WHAT'S N
Harper
DREW?

WHAT'S NEW

Harper

DREW?

Illustrated by
Aleksei Bitskoff

KATHY WEEKS

Hodder
Children's
Books

HODDER CHILDREN'S BOOKS

First published in Great Britain in 2022 by Hodder & Stoughton

3 5 7 9 10 8 6 4

Text copyright © Kathy Weeks, 2022
Cover and inside illustrations copyright © Aleksei Bitskoff, 2022

The moral rights of the author and illustrator have been asserted.

A CIP catalogue record for this book
is available from the British Library.

ISBN 978 1 444 96177 5

Printed and bound in Great Britain by Clays Ltd, Elcograf S.p.A.

The paper and board used in this book are made from
wood from responsible sources.

MIX
Paper from
responsible sources
FSC
www.fsc.org
FSC® C104740

Hodder Children's Books
An imprint of Hachette Children's Group
Part of Hodder & Stoughton Limited
Carmelite House
50 Victoria Embankment
London EC4Y 0DZ

An Hachette UK Company
www.hachette.co.uk

www.hachettechildrens.co.uk

For Evie and Teddy.

You Are Awesome.

THE DREW FAMILY ~~TREE~~ ~~WEED~~ PICK 'N' MIX

MY MUM'S BROTHER
UNCLE PAUL
PICK 'N' MIX:
gold chocolate coin

MOVIE PRODUCER. FLASH. LOOKS SHINY. A DEFINITE FAVOURITE.
But (a bit like his movies) nobody has ever seen one (in a pick 'n' mix).

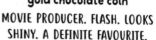

MAYBE A FRIEND, DEFINITELY IN THE COOL CREW
MAISIE FELIX
PICK 'N' MIX:
refresher chew

VERY POPULAR. LIKED BY EVERYONE. POTENTIALLY DANGEROUS.
You might dislocate your jaw.

BEST FRIEND FROM NEXT DOOR
PRIYA
PICK 'N' MIX:
gummy bear

BRIGHT. CUTE. SOFT.
Won't lose its head, even if stretched.

BEST FRIENDS SINCE WE WERE BORN
EDWARD
PICK 'N' MIX:
chocolate football

BRILLIANT. RELIABLE.
Always makes you feel better. First choice.

MY MUM
PICK 'N' MIX:
chocolate Brazil nut

NICE. GOOD FOR YOU.
TOTALLY NUTTY UNDERNEATH.

MY DAD
PICK 'N' MIX:
popping candy

SEEMS QUITE NORMAL.
But without any warning causes chaos
and mayhem and explosions. Everywhere.

HARPER DREW
PICK 'N' MIX:
fizzy cola bottle

STRONG. BUBBLY.
Mostly sweet, but
sometimes a bit too
fizzy to handle.

MY YOUNGER BROTHER
THE PRUNE
PICK 'N' MIX:
mini gem

HE'S SMALL BUT AWESOME.
I think he'll be the full
wine gum one day.

MY OLDER (& ANNOYING) BROTHER
TROY DREW
PICK 'N' MIX:
sherbet flying saucer

LOOKS GREAT ON THE OUTSIDE.
LOVED BY EVERYONE. BUT
DISAPPOINTING IN THE END.
Sherbet fizzles out too quickly.
And the rest tastes of cardboard.

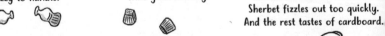

25 July

MY BIRTHDAY

AND THE FIRST DAY OF THE SUMMER HOLIDAYS

5.30 p.m.

Edward says that it wasn't a ***total disaster***.

But I think he is only trying to be nice. It was a COMPLETE *disaster*. A **GINORMOUS** hash-up. And that is me trying to look on the **bright** side.

I had been looking forward to my birthday for weeks. Because for the first time EVER my mum and dad agreed to a party that didn't involve my dad making **balloon sausage dogs** in our back garden. No, this year I was allowed to invite three whole friends to Laser Force at the shopping centre in town.

Maisie Felix had her birthday party there in January and it was **epic** *(apparently)*. But I didn't end up going . . . Although I did try my best. I'd spent ages getting ready

1

(new camouflage outfit and full combat face paint) and my mum dropped me off on **Sunday** at 2 p.m. Which was when I found out that the party had been on **Saturday** at 2 p.m. I had to wait in the gift shop talking to a shop assistant called Bernard until my mum came back to pick me up.

I'm not entirely sure how that happened (although a week later, my dad turned up a day late to meet his boss at work. He said he'd been using his calendar from last year to save money on buying a new one. So, I have my suspicions . . .)

I told Maisie that I missed her party because there had been a family emergency (which was totally believable knowing the Drew family). But I was pretty disappointed. Especially when it was all anyone could talk about at school – like the party had been the **best** day of their lives. **EVER**. It didn't help that the combat paint hadn't washed off my face quite as well as the bottle had said it would. I looked a muddy shade of green for about a week. After that, my brother Troy kept leaving his figure of **The Hulk** on my pillow every night.

So when Dad first suggested that I could have my party at Laser Force, I think he was feeling SOrry for me (either that or he was feeling **GUILTY** about being a cheapskate with his calendar, which made me miss Maisie's birthday). But whatever the reason . . . this was **HUGE** because:

1. It was Laser Force. Everyone (except me who had only ever been to the gift shop) **LOVED** Laser Force.

2. Not having to deal with the **balloon animal thing** I already mentioned. My dad started making them when we were toddlers and just can't seem to let them go. At last year's party Dad **burst 14 balloons** trying to make a chimpanzee. One balloon **exploded** right in Douglas Joiner's face.

He had to wear an eye patch for
three weeks.

3. I could invite Maisie Felix. (I am **desperate** for
an **invite** to her **summer glamping party** this
year and after my no-show at her birthday, I need
something **BIG** to get me back in her good books.)

I **wanted** to invite the whole class like Maisie had. But
according to my mum and dad, that would cost the same
as a new downstairs carpet, which we are seriously in
need of. So that was ruled out straight away and I had
to make do with **three** people.

This is what happened:

10.30 a.m.
TODAY was the day. I would have another go with
the camouflage outfit, saved from last time *(minus the
face paint)*.

I was ready from about **6.37 a.m.**

My dad had borrowed the school minibus so we could

4

all get there together. Which was **lucky**. Because the school *(where my dad teaches)* hadn't been willing to lend it to him for more than a year after an **INCIDENT** when he last borrowed it to take my grandad fishing. He parked up the minibus, and then couldn't remember where. It took him **TWO WHOLE** days to find it again. The school had to cancel **three football matches** and the biology field trip to a **frog farm**.

I **SO** wanted this day to be the best. And there had been **no** disasters so far. My best friend from next door, Priya, brought **FOUR** bags of FIZZY cola bottles *(the best of sweets, if you ask me)* on to the bus, and Edward, my best friend since we were born, was pouting at his reflection in the bus window. He was spiking his hair to look like my older brother Troy using Maisie Felix's orange juice, squeezing drops on to his hands out of the carton and sweeping his hair in upward motions to make it stick. I knew Edward would regret using the orange juice later. Two flies had flown into the bus and were already circling, checking out his head. And I had a bad feeling it was only a matter of time before several other members of this fly family arrived and started to swarm him.

Edward thinks Troy's hair routine is **ABSURD**. A full 10 out of 10 on a scale of RIDICULOUS things to be doing. Troy gets up 50 minutes earlier than me every day *(58 minutes earlier on a Saturday because of the extra wash)*. If you add all this time up, Troy is losing out on **38.88** whole nights of sleep. **EVERY YEAR**. Edward loves a lie-in. So he thinks Troy has totally **LOST THE PLOT**. And I have to agree with him.

Troy spends more time on his hair routine than a movie star probably does for a night out at the Oscars. Except the Oscars happen once a year. **Troy does it every day.**

The (hair) routine:

1. Wash twice. *Three times on a Saturday.* **(Why would it be dirtier on a Saturday?)**

2. Condition *(using my mum's expensive bottle she gets **especially** from the hairdresser and seems not to notice that it **mostly** ends up on **Troy's head**).*

3. Blow dry. *(Why use **one** hairdryer when you could use **two**? **One in each hand**.)*

4. Comb.

5. Brush *(apparently **4** and **5** are **TOTALLY** different and both **VERY** important).*

6. Comb again.

7. Gel.

8. Wax.

9. Twist. *(I mean . . . **what?**)*

10. Look lovingly into the mirror. *For **eight** whole minutes (**at least**).*

This is how the **DREW DIAL OF BIZARRE BEHAVIOUR** was born – with Troy's hair routine **(DREW DIAL RATING 10/10).** I started scoring other **ODD**, **WEIRD**, and totally RIDICULOUS things that seemed to go on around me. I didn't even have to look very hard. This stuff was happening **ALL THE TIME AND ALL OVER THE PLACE.** Most of the time it was like it was ONLY ME that could see it.

RATINGS ON THE DREW DIAL
Some examples:

DREW DIAL RATING 9/10: Our nativity play this year had been called *Elves Ruin Christmas.* Everyone was asked to come to school in **ELF COSTUMES** on the day of the show. Douglas Joiner's mum had read the instructions wrong and he came in dressed as **ELVIS. The singer.** Who had died like forty years ago. Is it just me? But . . . How did she not think she might have got this one wrong?

What on earth did she think *Elvis* had to do with the nativity? Me, Priya and Edward were laughing so much we couldn't go on stage for the first song. Miss Chester *(the music teacher)* made us clean the triangles at lunchtime as punishment.

DREW DIAL RATING 11/10: When my dad tried to PULL OUT my grandad's tooth with the front door. My grandad had had toothache for two weeks but refused to see an actual dentist because it was going to cost him **£62.10** to get the tooth taken out. Grandad said he *'wasn't going to pay that much money to come out with fewer teeth than he went in with'.* So my dad agreed to tie some plastic wire round the *dodgy* tooth, attach it to the front door and **SLAM** it. They thought the tooth would just pop out painlessly. It didn't. The wind blew the door closed at the wrong moment. The tooth CRACKED and my grandad covered the downstairs carpet in blood.

Which is why we are now saving for a new one *(carpet I mean, not a new grandad)*. It cost him double to fix the tooth at the dentist after all that.

DREW DIAL RATING 10/10: Priya's mum's cat royal family. This started at **8/10** when she got a Maine Coon cat called Prince Charles to go with her collection of plates and teapots with the Queen's face on them. But it is now a full on **10/10** since she added a very scratchy Prince William and then Kate Middleton to the cat family.

Did I mention, Priya's family is almost as unusual as

mine? I heard Priya's mum talking about getting a Princess Beatrice and Prince George the last time I was over there. I am worried that she isn't going to stop until she has the full line of succession. At which point, let's be honest, the **DREW DIAL RATING** will be **off the charts** – **A SOLID 17/10.**

In the end I was rating things so often in my head that I couldn't get much else done. The ratings were in **DANGER** of taking **longer** than Troy's hair routine. So I decided it would be easiest to give everyone their own individual **DREW DIAL RATING.** Like an overall score. A bit like the way you score gymnastics at the Olympics. You only get **one** mark but it covers the **whole** performance. The somersaults, how well they can do the splits and whether or not they **conk** their head when landing the final backflip.

The **DREW DIAL RATING** is sort of the same I guess. One mark out of ten. Looking at the whole performance ... but at **LIFE** (instead of gymnastics). On a scale of **0** to **10**, how likely is someone to SAY or DO something that would be less sensible than *(for example)* . . . *an out-of-control camel?*

CURRENT DREW DIAL RATINGS:

TROY: 9.9999/10. His hair remains a full **10/10**.

THE PRUNE: 3/10. My younger brother is six years younger than me and he is really **sweet**. He has a **massive** head and he **smiles** all the time and he seems *(so far at least)* to be the most **sensible** member of the Drew family. But he is still pretty young so there is time for that to change. But I hold out high hopes for him.

EDWARD: 0/10. I met him *(apparently)* when I was two days old and we have been **best friends** ever since. He is just **awesome**. No **chaos**. No

drama. No **mayhem**. He is just funny. And (sometimes stupidly) **kind**.

PRIYA: 2/10. Priya is BRILLIANT too and I feel a bit responsible for her **DREW DIAL RATING**. It is mainly not **0/10** because she ends up involved in my **HAVOC** and **MESS-UPS**. She lives next door so there's a lot of opportunities for her to get roped into the **Drew family mayhem**. Like when we had to be rescued by the fire brigade after we got locked inside my bedroom. It was **her idea**. But it was **my fault.**

MY MUM: 6.5/10 *(BUT IT MIGHT BE CREEPING UP).* She is mainly *brilliant* but likes THREE things way more than I think she should. *Maths, bleach* and *supermarkets* (but more on those later). **Not necessarily in that order.** We were late setting off for Laser Force because Mum hadn't finished bleaching the minibus. She was inside it **bleaching her bleach bottle (SERIOUSLY)** and we were all waiting outside, ready to go. She wasn't even coming with us *(to save money for the downstairs carpet)*. Although she did *try* her best to get a times-table competition going for the journey, but my dad just drove off, leaving her shouting, *'Six times seven?'* after us from the pavement.

MY DAD: 9/10. Dad is a **whole new level** to my mum. He always **means well** but seems to attract **MAYHEM** at the same rate as Edward's hair was now *attracting flies*. What I mean is, in a LARGE quantity.

EDWARD

10.45 a.m.

It turned out that today, my birthday, was going to be no exception. We rounded the corner to the shopping centre car park and were going down the ramp . . .

Apparently **Dad** had **forgotten** he was driving a minibus and thought he was in our family Nissan Qashqai. Which meant he **misjudged** the size of his

rear end, hit the curb and sent us **skidding**. We **crashed** into the ticket barrier and it

bent backwards. Dad began trying to reverse out of the disaster (as if it wasn't already bad enough).

Alarms started sounding – the barrier had gone through the passenger window.

'That police officer appears to be heading in our direction,' Edward pointed out.

Maisie Felix looked the most excited she had looked all day. Priya looked a **bit sick**.

'Hi, how are you? I'm Steve,' my dad said **breezily**

to the officer. As if he hadn't noticed the disaster he was sitting in. As if he thought he was talking to Priya's mum over the back fence at home about the progress of their courgette plants.

'Sir? I am not sure now is the right time to be talking about me,' said the officer dismissively. 'Let's focus on you. And how you appear to have made a metal kebab out of a minibus and a car-park ticket barrier.'

'I do love kebabs,' my dad shouted with a totally **inappropriate** level of enthusiasm, and it echoed around the car park. He got louder and carried on, 'Chicken usually, but spiced lamb is also . . .' His voice tailed off, probably because he'd noticed a fire engine pulling up behind us and finally realised that now was not the time to be discussing his ideal barbecue menu.

'**SIR!**' It was the police officer's turn to shout. Totally **appropriately**. 'Attempting to avoid paying to park your vehicle is a serious offence. Add in reckless driving, endangering the lives of four children – not to mention the damage to the ticket barrier – and I think that this is something we should be talking about down at the station.'

'The station?' came a voice from the fire engine somewhere behind us. 'You'll be waiting a while. It's going to take us hours to get him out of this mess. We'll have to use the laser.'

YOU HAD GOT TO BE KIDDING ME!

And so it was all over.

We missed our time slot at Laser Force while we waited for the fire brigade to use a **LASER (REALLY?** As if I needed reminding) to cut the barrier out of the minibus. It **took three hours**. And one of the fire fighters recognised us from the locked bedroom incident. If I still had the time to be rating every disaster on the Drew Dial . . . this one might have broken the scale.

During the wait my dad did manage to convince the police that it was **JUST AN ACCIDENT** and that he wasn't trying to pull a stunt to avoid paying the £4.55 cost of parking. Which was good. **But, also**

during the wait, Priya threw up *13 fizzy cola bottles* mixed with orange juice on to Maisie Felix.

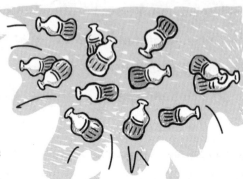

I had to give Maisie my camouflage outfit to change into. It was the only thing I could think that might save my invite to the glamping party.

2.45 p.m.

I got back home. Four hours later. **Smelling** of puke. **Wearing** my dad's jumper.

And I **STILL** haven't been to Laser Force.

*'That wasn't a **complete disaster**,'* Edward said, when he came over to mine for the birthday cake. But I think he just felt sorry for me. He even tried to convince me that the minibus journey had been fun,

which was when I knew he was **trying** to be nice *(the bit where we all nearly got skewered by a massive hunk of metal was definitely **not fun**)*. But he did stay to watch me open my presents, which I am pleased about.

So I opened the perfectly wrapped gift box from Maisie Felix. Everything about Maisie Felix is *(annoyingly)* perfect.

And inside it was **THIS** journal, which has these words in neon orange letters on the front:

I am not exactly sure what Maisie is trying to say about me.

But . . . she *might* be right.

27 July

THE DOWNSTAIRS CARPET

12 p.m.

After the birthday nightmare I wasn't sure that I would write anything more in here.

But I have been thinking about it, and maybe Maisie does have a point with this journal. Because quite often **. . . I *DO* . . . HAVE *NO* IDEA WHAT IS GOING ON.** Like I am living in a world full of chaos and mayhem. Surrounded by people doing bizarre things that don't make **ANY** sense. **At all.** And I can't understand why I seem to be the **ONLY ONE** who sees all of this for what it is. Completely **BEYOND** normal.

So I am going to write some of this stuff down. **HERE.** As a record of all of the **mayhem** and **eye-rolls** and **head-screams** *(you know, where you want to* **SCREAM OUT LOUD***, but that will only make the chaos worse, so you* SCREAM *in your mind instead).*

Because I reckon that with a journal of these things that are happening all around me, I will be able to look back after I have stopped **head-screaming** *(and my eyes have returned from my eyebrows)* and **check whether . . . it really is just me?**

And if I ever need to, I can show this journal to someone else. For a second opinion. And then they can be the judge of whether they agree with my **DREW DIAL RATINGS . . .**

So I started with the birthday incident and thinking about it again did make me feel quite sorry for my dad. He has been pretty down the last few days and keeps apologising for ruining my birthday. He even spelt out the word 'sorry' using animal modelling balloons.

It took **25 balloons** which he says is the most he has ever used since he taught himself how to do them *(when he recreated the whole of Noah's Ark in balloon animals* *for Troy's first birthday).* So Dad must be **REALLY** sorry. After all, he only borrowed the minibus for the Laser Force trip, and now he is down £652, which is how much it'll cost to fix the passenger window and replace the ticket barrier. Dad hoped it would be covered on the insurance . . . but it isn't. Apparently *'being a terrible driver'* isn't something they'll pay for.

I don't I think I'll be going to Laser Force again any time soon . . . we are banned from the car park anyway.

And getting a new downstairs carpet is off.

28 July

ITCHY TEETH

My invite to Maisie Felix's summer glamping party hasn't arrived yet. **Fingers crossed** it is still in the post, but Edward got his yesterday. So things aren't looking hopeful on that front. Priya hasn't got one either. Which might have something to do with the cola bottles she **spewed up** over Maisie last week.

The party happens every summer in Maisie's **HUGE** garden, which is just round the corner from our *(very much smaller)* garden. Last year I didn't get invited after a misunderstanding about some peanuts. I was **trying** to be **NICE**. I gave Maisie most of my packet. I thought that they had *(generously)* come from Daniel Muldoon. Which they had. It just turned out that he had **found them** piled up outside a Chinese takeaway on the way to school. He had been generously giving them out at break time. But on closer inspection the use by date was basically **LAST CENTURY** . . .

so not quite so generous after all. Everyone felt ill that afternoon. Especially Maisie. She said she was sick for a **whole week**. And so I had to **watch** the glamping party from our bathroom window.

Maisie had these big coloured tepees and sparkling lights. And everyone *(and I mean everyone, except me)* stayed over for **two whole days**. It was *(apparently)* the BEST thing that happened in the summer holidays. At least that is what Maisie said. And if Maisie says so, everyone usually thinks it is true.

She even called it

MAISIE'S FABULOUS FESTIVAL

and the letters **MFF** were all over everything. The cakes. The bunting. Even the burgers had **MFF** stamped on them. Although that was a **mistake**. Her dad had accidentally bought vegan burgers from the **Meat Free Food Company**. Douglas Joiner thought it would be funny to stuff an open packet of vegan burgers in Sarah

Utal's sleeping bag. But he got the wrong one and the next morning Maisie Felix woke up looking like she had showered using a *(vegan)* lasagne instead of soap. And a sticker with the words '**Meat Free Food**' was attached to her **bottom**. Douglas Joiner had to eat lunch on his own with only Maisie's dog on the second day. I bet he isn't invited this year.

If it had been my festival *(which it won't ever be because our garden is about the size of 17½ postage stamps and has no grass)*, I wouldn't have dared call it a **'Fabulous Festival'** before it had even started. I think it is asking for trouble because how can you be sure it will be *fabulous* until it is over and has **ACTUALLY** been *fabulous*?

And now, just thinking about this invite is giving me **itchy teeth**.

Which is annoying because I thought things were looking promising at the end of last term.

The **Triple Threat** *(that's me, Edward and Priya)* were on our way home from school. I've never called us

the **Triple Threat** out loud of course . . . but I kind
of like to think of us as that. We're good on our own,
but together we are a force to be reckoned with
(something like that anyway).

We were going past Maisie's house, which takes quite a
while because her house is massive. *(It has two front
doors. Who needs a spare front door?)* While Priya and
Edward went on ahead, I may have
stopped for a short minute to look
up at the new **gold wallpaper**
that I could see through the front
windows. I was wondering if it
might ACTUALLY have **diamonds** in it because
with all the **sparkle** in my eyes I think I was
HYPNOTISED. Just **staring** at the wallpaper . . .

Which . . . was when . . . Maisie saw me.

From her bedroom window.

Amelie and Amelia *(Maisie's best friends)* were up

there too. Of course they were. It's like those two have been stapled to her. Maisie calls them the **AA**. As if she owns them. I have never worked out whether she realises that the **AA** is also the name of a company that fixes broken-down cars. Maybe she does . . . because the **AA** are always around whenever Maisie's **'warning lights'** start to flash (aka a **diva drama** is about to happen over something serious like eating the wrong peanut or not being first in line for lunch).

'Do you want something, Harper? You've been out there for ages,' Maisie shouted from her window.

NIGHTMARE.

And also, **not true**. At least, I don't think so anyway.

How long *had* I been staring at the wallpaper?

A while, obviously. Edward and Priya were already at the door to my house. I watched my mum let them in and saw through the kitchen window her giving them a lemonade. I thought about why no one wondered where I was . . . but then I remembered that **Maisie** and the **AA** were watching.

I dived down and pretended to be doing up my laces. Which was a **BAD** move. Because then I couldn't get up. If I did, they would see that my shoes didn't have any laces that needed tying. I'd taken them out a few weeks ago to help when the elastic in my gym shorts decided to go into early retirement just before PE started.

'We're just setting up my new phone,' Maisie carried on from her window. *'Give me your number and I'll add you to the chat group for the festival.'*

This **MUST** mean I **WAS** getting an invite. For a moment, I almost jumped for joy. But then I remembered I couldn't jump for joy *(or any other reason)* because then they'd see I was tying imaginary shoe laces. And then . . . I remembered that this was classic Maisie.

Did she **really** want me in the chat group? Or did she just want to let me know that she knows I don't have a phone? Who knows . . . These are the Maisie Felix mind games I am dealing with!

And this is the problem. **This is why my teeth itch**.

You are just never quite sure where you stand with Maisie Felix. **Sometimes** she can be super friendly. Usually when she wants to eat your peanuts or borrow your homework. But **then** she can decide you are a loser. And this often happens **SEVERAL** times in the same day.

So she really does seem to 'rule'. I can't really explain it, but whatever she does, wears, says or even thinks gets everyone in a **massive frenzy** trying to copy her. Douglas Joiner spent his whole allowance on the same watch strap as Maisie. But he couldn't afford the actual smartwatch that it went with (which Maisie has, obviously). He had to Sellotape the strap to his old watch, and I am not sure it looked as good as he had hoped.

In the end, life is all just a bit easier if you are on **Team Maisie**. And SHE picks the team. The problem is, she also dangles the threat of the subs bench at every possible opportunity. And the idea of being dropped from the side . . . well, it just isn't worth the hassle.

'Er. Yeah. My number. It's . . . er . . .' I needed to think fast. I needed a pretend phone number and I needed to get up off the floor – my legs had gone seriously numb. So I gave Maisie Priya's number, and as she was typing it into her phone I crawled on to a wall next door to try to deal with the pins and needles that had spread as far as my hips.

'Awesome,' Maisie called after me. I heard the AA laughing as she said, 'I'll put you in as "Princess".'

And there it was **AGAIN**. Classic Maisie.

She KNOWS that I am trying my hardest to ditch the Princess nickname. But she seems to think it is hilarious. And, because **she** thinks it is **hilarious**, guess what . . . **everyone** else does too.

It has been going on for over a month now. It started when Daniel Muldoon and James Merrison told me I was a *total* dork because I asked Mrs Travers three questions in our English lesson. They called me a **dork** for a week. And then moved on to '**Harper, Princess of Dorkness**'. And then just '**Princess**'. I thought they were pretty mean . . . I was **FAIRLY SURE** no one else had a clue what a possessive pronoun was, so why not ask Mrs Travers? They decided that this made me a huge loser, but *(and here is another question)* what is the point in wasting seven whole hours a day at school if you come out less intelligent than before you went in? And that is looking likely for Daniel Muldoon and James Merrison. Once they were limbo dancing under the desks in Mr Winwood's maths lesson while he went to the cupboard to get some protractors. They cracked their heads together going backwards under the same desk. James Merrison now says he's lost his memory and that is why he can't do times tables.

And they think *I* am the dork? **Seriously?**

When I finally got back home I was a bit dizzy. I couldn't work out whether it was the pins and needles or that I was still hypnotised by Maisie's sparkly wallpaper. Edward and Priya were eating jam sandwiches and watching *Countdown* with my mum *(she loves the numbers round, of course)*. When I told them about Maisie, Edward said I shouldn't care about the Princess thing. He said everyone will have forgotten about it by the end of the holidays.

He was right. As usual.

But every time I hear the **'P'** word, my teeth start to itch. And itchy teeth are the **WORST**. Think about having a mouthful of **really hairy** spiders . . . **eeeurghhhhhhh**, just thinking about it makes my teeth go **weird.** That is what itchy teeth feels like.

And it is happening again now. Every time I think about the invite to Maisie's party.

29 July

THE WIG

1.00 p.m.

Uncle Paul *(current* **DREW DIAL RATING 11/10** *but this is always moving – upwards)* came round to give me my birthday present.

Which also meant Dad has been acting weird. And by that, I mean weirder than usual.

Uncle Paul is *(apparently)* a movie producer. But I would have thought that a movie producer would have to . . . well . . . **produce some movies?** But as far as I can tell, no one has ever even seen a YouTube clip that he's made, **let alone a whole film.**

But this doesn't stop my dad from thinking that every meetup with Uncle Paul is a potential audition for a part in Uncle Paul's next *(or, if everyone is being really honest, first)* HOLLYWOOD BLOCKBUSTER. I am not entirely sure what part my dad thinks he might be trying out for, but this **'auditioning'** usually involves some kind of superhero pose *(often on just one leg)*, and a hard stare into the distance followed by some meaningful words, in the deepest voice he can possibly manage, like **'The world needs help . . .'**

Today, he actually did a forward roll into the kitchen while my mum and uncle Paul were having a cup of tea.

But this is my dad. And he **BANGED** his head on the tiled floor and then couldn't get up. I think he said **'Avengers Assemble'** from under the table but the **squeal** was so **high pitched** I can't quite be sure.

To be fair to Uncle Paul, producing movies is a fairly recent thing. Up until two years ago he was an estate agent. But he had to leave that job when there was a mix-up *(his words)* after a family came home from a trip to the local zoo to find Uncle Paul **ASLEEP** on their sofa. He said he was **PLUMPING** up the cushions to make the house look nice. They said he was **SNORING**.

So he was asked to leave. The house. And the estate agency job.

I felt sorry for Uncle Paul when that happened. If he had been tired *(which he says he definitely wasn't)* then it was only because he also had a night job driving a taxi back then. **Leonardo DiCaprio** *(his **dog**, not the **famous actor**)* had got ill and the vet bills were so expensive he needed an extra job to pay for the treatment.

So, a few weeks after the end of his estate agent career, and with a very **dramatic** change in hairstyle, he announced that he was producing a movie and that he had Chris Hemsworth parked up in a trailer by the local park ready to start filming.

Really? Is it that **easy** to become the next Steven Spielberg?

And I think my mum was doubtful too, although she did say that Uncle Paul had always had **big dreams**. Ever since he was an extra in two episodes of *Coronation Street* when he was nine. Apparently they told him that he was the **best** child extra they had ever had. He still sees it as his biggest achievement and tells everyone who will listen that he was a total **natural**.

It seems odd to me to be proud of being a 'natural' extra. Surely that is like saying you are brilliant at blending into the background?

Anyway, **that** isn't the only thing that's odd:

*1. His new **hairstyle** is **something** else. The amount of hair he has **doubled overnight**. He can't have grown it that fast, so it's either a **wig** or one of those **hair transplants**. Where they take hairs from your **big toe** (or something like that) and implant them on your head. Either way, Troy* has been **wild** with **jealousy** and trying to figure out how Uncle Paul is able to style in so much **'volume'**.

2. Then there's the **diamond ring** he started wearing. **On his thumb**. (Is that a **thing** in Hollywood?) I don't know if it is real or not, but it's **huge**.

3. The **new car**. A **bright orange Ferrari**. Dad keeps joking that Beyoncé must be wanting her car back. It is pretty **cool**, but quite how he had the money to pay for it is a total mystery. And it looks seriously **out of place** parked outside his two-bedroom bungalow next to his neighbour's 14-year-old Ford Fiesta.

4. And then let's not forget the **trailer**, with Chris Hemsworth in it.

Priya's mum drove us past the park on the way back from school one day. And there was a small **campervan** there. But I don't think Chris Hemsworth was in it. It just didn't **look** like the kind of **trailer** a **Hollywood star** would be hanging out in. One of the windows was cracked and there seemed to be a plant growing out of the roof. And anyway, it's been two years since then, Uncle Paul hasn't mentioned Chris since and . . . as far as I know . . . **there is no movie**.

Uncle Paul is one of the most generous people I have ever met. He gave me an iPhone two years ago. (*But my mum wouldn't let me keep it. I still don't have a phone*). Then a flat-screen TV last year. (*Which is now in our sitting room as the 'family' TV.*)

But he looked a bit sheepish when he handed over the envelope to me today. At the time I thought that maybe he was worried my mum was going to be annoyed with how generous he was being. But I don't think that was it. Because when I opened it up *(hoping for tickets to Disneyland Florida)*, it was empty except for a **photo** of Uncle Paul and **Leonardo DiCaprio** *(the dog, not the actor).*

THIS WILL BE WORTH A FORTUNE ONE DAY.
LOVE, UNCLE PAUL

He'd even signed it: I have a feeling that day might be quite a while away, but I gave him a giant hug anyway.

2 August

CHICKPEAS

It has been a fairly peaceful couple of days in the Drew household. It is the calm before the storm though. Actually, a storm would be way too mild – **THIS** will be more like a HURRICANE, **TYPHOON**, **EARTHQUAKE** and **TSUNAMI** rolled into one. **THIS** being the **annual family holiday** to France. Happening in two days' time. And while there will be about a **million** problems to deal with when me, the Prune, Troy and his hair have to sit together in the back of the car for **17 hours**, I can't focus on that right now.

Because . . . I've just checked with Priya and she was **not** added to Maisie's party chat group. I **knew** Maisie was playing mind games with me.

And there is **STILL** no invite. Even Douglas Joiner has got one now. Apparently, he cleaned Maisie's dad's cars *(he has three)* and let Maisie pretend she had done it. This is looking **very bad. Teeth. Very. Itchy**.

Edward says I have **FOMO** *(fear of missing out)*. But it isn't quite that. I actually think I have **FOAMO**. This is not a new type of soap. **FOAMO** = *fear of ANYONE missing out*. I just **don't like it** when **anyone** is left out.

I guess it is because I have seen the way that Edward gets **left out** of loads of things. And it makes me **SO mad**.

Edward uses a wheelchair to get around. He has something called cerebral palsy. It was probably caused by a problem with his brain just before he was born. There is **NOTHING** wrong with Edward's brain now though. He is the smartest kid I know. But his **legs** and **arms** don't work *quite as well* as they should. So he gets left out of things. **ALL THE TIME**. Maisie didn't invite him to Laser Force because she thought they wouldn't have access for his chair. **They did though**. She just didn't even **bother** to ask.

Edward even had to have a science lesson on his own at school a couple of weeks ago. The science labs are up some **really steep steps** – seriously, even with rock-climbing gear they'd be **risky**. So he has no chance in his wheelchair. There **is** a stairlift, **but** it keeps **breaking down** and last week it came to a COMPLETE STOP. And while the rest of the class were experimenting with conical flasks and potassium permanganate, Edward had to have his lesson *under the stairs* in the science block, learning the periodic table from a textbook.

It's not **FAIR** that he can't even get into the classroom. Edward wants to be a **doctor** and I am worried that this broken stairlift might hamper his chances. I also really want Edward in the class, if I am honest. It's better to have him around. Some of the other kids are WILD up there. Joseph Johnson **burned** one of Sarah Utal's **eyebrows** off last term. Apparently his excuse was that his Bunsen burner *'went rogue'*. It hasn't grown back. **The eyebrow**.

Anyway, it looks like the only solution to Edward's science problem is a **new** stairlift. So for the last few months it has been my mission to raise enough to buy one. I've looked into it closely. And we need £5,500 for the **cheapest** model *(apparently this one doesn't have a handrail but we'll have to live without that)*. We also have to raise the money by Christmas so we can buy it in the January sale where they give you 20% off *(plus a free cushion)*.

Everyone has said they will help raise the money.

Even Troy.

But . . . Troy's efforts so far have been . . . typical of Troy . . .

Take his **BIG** announcement from yesterday – that he was starting a **skateboarding vlog**.

'When it goes viral, Harper, I'll buy the stairlift,' he said, with all the confidence of someone who might run a medium-sized country.

REALLY? . . . **WHEN** it goes viral?

This is yet another hopeless idea because . . . and this is the typical Troy bit . . .

TROY DOESN'T EVEN OWN A SKATEBOARD.

So in what world? **Is ANYONE?** Going to **want** to **watch** him **spewing total nonsense** about rail slides, ollies and getting air?

They aren't.

But despite this *(clearly massive)* problem for Troy's new **'career'** *(his words, not mine)*, he seems to think that this is the **BEST IDEA** he has ever had. And believe me, this is the latest in a long line of his **'BEST'** ideas.

With **NO** skill, **NO** clue and **NO** skateboard, he really thinks that kids across the globe are going to subscribe to his channel in their millions and make him **rich** beyond his **WILDEST** dreams. **Instantly.**

They just aren't.

But this is the way Troy approaches everything in his life. Not much effort *from* him, and very high expectations of the benefits *for* him. And yet, despite his total lack of commitment to anything except his hairstyle, **EVERYONE** *(including Troy)* **loves Troy.**

He is two years older than me. For some reason that I can't work out, the kids at school think he is seriously cool. And he is, for sure, my parents' favourite child. They would never say that of course. But it is obvious.

For a start, his name is **Troy**. TROY! **Who gets called Troy? Superheroes** mostly, that's who. My parents must have believed that Troy would grow up to rescue the planet from whatever war, natural disaster or other hot mess would be going on at the time (*while always maintaining his* perfect *hairstyle*). Why else would you call a kid from a small, three-bedroom, semi-detached house in a very ordinary cul-de-sac **TROY**?

None of his other recent '**BEST**' ideas have done anything to dampen my parents' adoration either. Last month he announced he was going to '*get Edward the new stairlift*' (*Troy's words again*) by selling a **new** type of baked beans to the local neighbourhood. Generously (*although not that generously at all*) he offered Edward's stairlift fund a whole 10% of the profits.

At least this time he was trying to make (*some*) money for Edward **BUT** . . . and here comes typical Troy again . . .

Like **ANYONE** needs a *'new type'* of baked beans? As usual, he hadn't given this plan any thought. If he had, he would have remembered that Heinz have pretty well got the bean market covered. But, not one to be put off by an existing, tasty, multi-million-dollar global competitor, Troy decided to fill some old jam jars with chickpeas covered in ketchup. He didn't even wash the jam jars out first, his effort level was so low.

As usual, my mum and dad thought this was one of the most **amazing** endeavours of all time. *'So enterprising,'* my dad said proudly while my mum drove Troy from street to street to help him peddle the **lumpy gunk**.

And this is what is **SO** annoying. About Troy.

WHY WAS I the only one who thought that this was

going to be a complete waste of Mum's time and the family petrol budget?

WHY WAS I the only one to suggest *(by which I mean screaming in my own head)* that *'OMG, CHICKPEAS ARE NOT EVEN BEANS!'*?

And WHY WAS I the only one to see that the people in our neighbourhood, which isn't exactly full of ten-bedroom mansions *(apart from Maisie's)*, were not likely to spend their money on a dirty jar of slime almost certain to cause death by food poisoning?

These are questions that I still can't find answers to.

IS IT JUST ME?

Am I the ONLY one who can see the flaws in Troy's schemes? Because while I am thinking he is *(much)* less sensible than an out-of-control camel . . . everyone else always looks at him as if he is the best thing to happen to the world since Disney released that song called *'Let It Go'*.

Now, don't get me wrong, I am all for trying something new. And I like a money-making invention as much as they do over at Apple iPhone. But what makes me frustrated is that no one else seems to see Troy for what he is . . . which is:

Totally useless. **BUT,** and here is the thing, if he **actually** bothered to do **ANYTHING properly** he'd probably be the **world's youngest billionaire**.

Even his best friend Frankie wouldn't buy any of the beans. He had one taste and then asked for a double refund because he couldn't feel his tongue any more.

So in case you were wondering about **Troyz Beanz** (yes, that's really what he called them), he managed precisely **ZERO** sales.

And **10%** of zero is . . . no extra money for the stairlift ☹.

6 August

THE JOURNEY
PART ONE

12.45 p.m.

I am finding Troy **TOO** annoying to look at today. He has somehow bought himself half a skateboard. **Only** Troy could buy **50%** of a skateboard. He got it second-hand online and didn't bother to look at the photos. The bottom half was always mysteriously out of shot. When it arrived, it only had **two** wheels.

That hasn't dampened Troy's enthusiasm though. He has spent the last two hours **talking to himself** *(while holding his skateboard, **top half only**)* in the mirror. This is VLOG practice. And apparently that gets you out of having to help pack the car for the family holiday.

There's **STILL** no invite from Maisie Felix. I am

beginning to think I should make other plans. Daniel Muldoon is even going now, according to Priya. He went round to Maisie's house with a box of doughnuts and Maisie's mum invited him on the spot. **Genius idea**. I wish I had thought of that.

But the itchy teeth are going to have to go on hold for a while because today is the start of the family holiday.

I LOVE the family holiday.

This year I am excited to start teaching the Prune how to *Lilo Loaf*. This is a great game invented by my dad. He is always coming up with new games. Some are better *(and safer)* than others. Priya has not been allowed over to our house since she needed four stitches after a life-threatening game Dad invented called *Kitchen Cabinet Long Jump*. She was all set to win too. But instead of jumping off the kitchen cabinets as far as she could and landing on the floor, Priya got her foot caught in the sink. She crashed down on to the toaster and had to go straight to A & E for stitches in her left elbow. We only meet up at her house now.

Lilo Loafing is a (slightly) safer holiday game Dad thought of last year. You get up and stand tall on the lilo while it floats in the water. The **winner** is the person who manages to stand on the lilo for the longest without falling in. **Last year I was the winner.** Troy wouldn't even give it a go. He was too worried he would get his **hair wet**. My dad was **HOPELESS** and couldn't even get on to his knees before falling off. I pipped my mum in the final, but it was close.

This year, Dad is suspiciously confident. I think that he has been secretly practising at the local pool.

He goes for a swim twice a week before school and the other day I found a pink lilo on the back seat of the car with his swimming goggles.

Anyway . . . the holiday is something to look forward to, and now that the Prune is older it will be fun to get him involved too.

But we have the issue of the 18-hour journey to get there. Which always brings out maximum readings on the **DREW DIAL** from all family members *(except me and the Prune, of course)*. This year is going to be no different.

Departure time is ALWAYS supposed to be 1 p.m. And **every** year we **miss** it. Because the packing of the car is always **BEDLAM**. This year, by 12.45 p.m. the only items in the car were **five** bottles of bleach.

 Is it just me? . . . But they DO have bleach in France, right? But my mum can't take the risk. She doesn't relax until she has done a complete round of the *'gite'* (aka a small French cottage in the middle of nowhere) with the Domestos.

Then, as if we had all of the time in the universe, she asked me a maths question.

'Harper, if the car boot is one and a half metres wide, how many bottles of bleach could I get across the back if each bottle has a width of five centimetres?' This was what she was actually asking me at 12.47 p.m. I would have thought that she might have more pressing issues on her mind (like we were going to miss the ferry for the fourth year in a row) but apparently not. She even waited and did her annoying clicky fingers thing. Like I was on a timer and my whole future success in life depended on getting the answer. I said 30. Which made me worry that she has another 25 bottles of bleach she plans to add to the five already in the car.

Mum came back out of the house carrying a seriously **heavy** box. The extra 25 bottles of bleach? But I should have known – it was the tins.

So . . . my mum loves a supermarket. In a happy coincidence, my mum does actually work for a supermarket. Sadly, she doesn't work in the actual supermarket shop though. She works at head office. Which means that at every possible opportunity *(and at many other non-opportunities)* she wants to go to a supermarket. Let's just say . . . if she could live on the cold meat counter or have her birthday party in the ketchup aisle, she would.

And because Mum works in the non-fresh produce department, she gets discount on mainly tinned items. And a two week holiday is *(apparently)* a perfect time to take full advantage of the 25% saving on 14 cans of chicken chasseur and 14 cans of beef bourguignon.

Now, is it just me, but what is the point in driving for 18 hours to the south of France only to eat French food from a tin that you brought with you from your local English supermarket? But that is what we will be doing.

When all of the stuff had been loaded into the boot, it wouldn't close. Which meant that there had to be a discussion *(argument)* about what we wouldn't be able to take after all. My vote would have been to **DITCH** the tins of French food. Seeing as . . . you know . . . we could probably *(definitely)* get those there. Or even better, **DITCH** Troy . . . seeing as that would free up a whole **chunk** of extra space especially if you took his hair into account.

But nobody asked me.

There was a stand-off between Troy, who refused to take out nine different kinds of moisturising shampoo, and my dad, who secretly smuggled in an extra lilo *(which I suspect was the one he has been practising with all year)*.

In the end, my mum decided to be *'the bigger person'* and removed three pairs of high heels she put in. All in their **individual** shoeboxes. She said they were for *'a nice night out in a French restaurant'*. Which also means that they were totally **unnecessary**.

She has clearly been dreaming. We have never ever had one of those nights out on a French holiday. **EVER**. Because my dad would never let us waste the tins and we always take so many with us there is hardly the chance of a shop-bought croissant, let alone the kind of night out that might need three pairs of high heels.

2.15 p.m.

We have left. **FINALLY**. And as usual there was a frantic call to the ferry company to see if there was a space on a later ferry. We were in luck, but one year the answer was no, and we had to sleep in the car at the port until the next morning. Everything was shut by the time we arrived so we had to crack open four tins of fish bouillabaisse *(French stew)* so we didn't starve. That was a night I am still trying to forget.

And with the *(real)* possibility that it could happen again, surely it would have made sense to pack the car the night before. But that seems to be a risk my dad can't take *(like my mum and all the bleach)*. He is too worried that someone will steal the car with all our holiday gear in it.

I think this is unlikely. After all, what thief is likely to want: ⬇

a **10-year-old Nissan Qashqai** (with 47 scratches. My mum counts every time my dad gets a new one),

24 tins of meat,

enough bleach to clean the whole of the city of Birmingham,

a **shampoo selection** for the entire cast of *Britain's Next Best Model,*

and **four suitcases** filled with the Drew family swimsuits.

Seriously?

2.36 p.m. and 42 seconds

We had only been in the car for 21 minutes and 42 seconds. We hadn't even started the Drew family-car-journey music rotation. **Then it happened.**

I wasn't surprised. It was **always** going to happen. It always **DID** happen. I could see the glint in my mum's eye as we approached the roundabout.

The one with the turn-off to the supermarket.

The dreaded words *'we could do with a baguette for the journey'* were uttered, and the next thing I knew we were reversing into one of the world's smallest spaces in the supermarket car park.

Now, is it just me, but when you have already missed one ferry and are 40 minutes behind schedule for the next one, is it sensible to stop off for a stick of French bread? At the supermarket next to your house? When the ferry you are going to miss . . . IS GOING TO THE LAND OF FRENCH BREAD?

But for my mum, this is quite normal behaviour.

She is in some kind of weird and never-ending loop.

She is always either on her way to, way back from or planning her next trip to . . . the supermarket. These trips can happen day or night. On the way to a holiday, to school, after school, at the weekend, between swimming practices and once during a clarinet lesson. Mr Ferrier (the clarinet teacher) had broken his leg and we were doing the lesson on video call instead. What better moment, thought Mum, than now to pack me, the iPad and the clarinet into the back of the car and 'pop out to pick up a couple of pints of milk'. Though I think my mum regretted that trip. I got car sick and threw up all over Mr Ferrier **(VIRTUALLY)** and all over my clarinet **(ACTUALLY)**.

The other problem is that she only ever buys two grocery items at a time. Which means we are always running out of stuff.

Does she not realise that the whole purpose of a trolley is to allow you to purchase more than the items you can carry with just your two bare hands?

Obviously, I already know the answer to that

question. She realises, all right, but if she does actually make use of a trolley and fill it with enough items for a seven-day stretch, a complete family meal, or a full two-week holiday, it will take away her chance of six other supermarket visits this week. And she won't cope well with that. In fact, her mood **dips dramatically** if she goes **more** than 48 hours without visiting a salad aisle.

So we are all stuck in this **never-ending** loop of supermarket trips with her.

And this one was no exception. **Maximum mayhem**. As usual.

Mum, the Prune and I got out to go to the supermarket. The parking space was so tight that Dad and Troy couldn't get out of the car. My dad was so pleased with this result, I wonder if he had planned it.

2.45 p.m.

I want to stop calling him the Prune, but I can't help it. When he came home from hospital after he was born, he was so small and shrivelled that I thought he looked like a little wrinkly **raisin**. As he got bigger that name didn't seem appropriate, so I started calling him the **Prune** instead *(a slightly bigger and less wrinkly dried fruit)*. And the name stuck. And now almost everyone calls him the **Prune**, which is fine with me, but I do worry about what the kids in his class might make of this when he starts school. His real name is James. My mum and dad clearly got less and **less ambitious** with the baby names after Troy. I guess that already having one son who's destined to save the world is **QUITE ENOUGH** for any family.

After the obligatory trip to the cereal aisle *(non-fresh produce)* so that my mum could report back to head office that all boxes were **correctly** displayed facing outwards *(or something like that)*, she picked up a baguette and headed for the till.

And then . . . Mum realised that she had lost the Prune.

She started running up and down the aisles with the baguette in her hand like an oversized relay baton. When she really started to panic she decided the baguette was holding her back and so she thrust it into the hands of the guy stacking lemons in the fruit section. He looked very confused, probably because he wasn't sure whether to join in the search for the Prune or take the baguette and start sprinting his leg of a 400m relay.

Now . . . is it just me?

But how hard is it to remember how many children you have?

Because this was not the first time that this had happened. In fact, this was the second time this week!

My mum and dad went to the cinema at the weekend. They got a new babysitter through an app called BabySquat. When the babysitter arrived my mum told her that her children were watching TV and were not allowed any more sweets, then quickly left the house. She forgot to add that she also had another child who had already hit the hay upstairs.

Three hours later, the babysitter (*convinced that the house was haunted*) called my parents to help her solve the mystery of the screeching wails from behind the door of the back bedroom.

'*Oh, but that's just James,*' my mum explained to the baffled babysitter – who had been on the verge of calling the local vicar and arranging an emergency exorcism. '*Did I forget to mention him?*'

YES, I wanted to scream into my pillow. How can you forget to mention one of your three offspring? If maths was as important as she made us think it was, counting to three should not be **THIS** hard!

So when it happened again in the supermarket, my heart sank. Apart from the fact we were almost certain to miss the ferry now, I knew exactly what would happen next. My mum would start to scream, the tannoy would be deployed and everyone in the supermarket would start pointing at us.

In fairness to Mum, I hadn't noticed she had lost him either. But then, I wasn't the parent in all this (*although I sometimes feel I might make a better go of it*). I had actually been distracted by of one of her maths questions and had been working out the cash saving on four tubs of cottage cheese that had been reduced by 30%.

The Prune was found safe and well back in the cereal aisle. In tears. Clutching a large box of Coco Pops. I guess he'd figured there was a possibility my mum might never notice he was missing. So he had picked the best cereal and the one my mum never lets us eat. And, **amazingly**, she bought it for him. The kid isn't stupid.

With a great sense of relief, we picked up a bag of French bonbons (*my mum gets a discount on those too*) and headed back out to the car park. It wasn't much less chaotic in the car though. My dad and Troy were having a thumb war. But my dad was leaning so far into the back seat to wrestle, his knee had turned the hazard lights on and was now pressing firmly on the horn. He hadn't even noticed and a security guard had started to cordon off the car with shopping trolleys while shouting, *'Stand back, we have a situation!'* to passers-by.

Seriously?

It wasn't until we got halfway down the motorway that I realised we had left the baguette behind.

5.30 p.m. – Fish Eyes

Surprisingly we **ALMOST** made it to the ferry on time. I think my dad was driving too fast during my mum's choice on the Drew family-music rotation. It was like he thought that if he drove faster, my mum's songs (*always four by Take That and one by Celine Dion*) would be over sooner. She was so busy belting out the words to the *Titanic* theme tune she didn't notice his speed.

But *(unsurprisingly)* things went sideways when we were only 400 metres from the port. My dad **missed** the turning off the roundabout. **Twice.** On the third time around, he must have been dizzy or delirious from listening to Troy's favourite grime song for the fifth time on repeat. Whatever the problem was, Dad went the wrong way.

Straight into a major traffic jam.

It was bad. A lorry carrying frozen fish had had some kind of a back-door malfunction and spilled what looked *(and smelled)* like three million mackerel all over the road ahead of us. We must have arrived **right after** it had happened because the lorry driver had just got down from his cab and was calling for help. I thought that phoning the police would have been a better idea. But instead he was knee deep in fish and just shouting °ⒽⒺⓁⓅ!° madly down the road. The fish must have been seriously *slippery* because he just couldn't stay upright. He kept falling face first into the mackerel and was covered in fish slime.

This was going to be a long wait.

Which was when I started thinking that if we were ever going to get through this, we needed to do something.

Troy said he wouldn't get out of the car because he was worried that his hair might absorb the smell of mackerel. My dad said he couldn't either, because of his *'phobia of fish eyes'*. Which he says started when he had to dissect one in science at school and it *'popped without warning'*. He hasn't been able to walk past a fishmonger's since he was 14.

Me and mum went to see if we could do anything for the lorry driver who was clearly in a complete panic. He told us that he only gets paid if he delivers 98% of his goods successfully. So I could see his problem. Because that was definitely not happening now.

Obviously, this prompted Mum to ask me a maths question about how many of his two thousand fish *(it turned out to be slightly less than three million)* he would need to deliver to qualify for his money.

The answer was 1960 and it wasn't a tricky one by her standards . . . But, is it just me . . . or are there SO many more questions that we should have been asking?

LIKE . . .

Why had no one called the police/fire brigade/fish brigade . . . or whoever . . . but someone who could help move these fish?

AND . . .

How long before these fish would defrost into an even bigger slimy mess? It was 37 degrees out here.

AND . . .

Why was it OK that he didn't deliver two out of

every hundred of these fish?

The lorry driver had fallen over again, and this time he had dropped his phone into the sea of fish. After we'd helped him up, I suggested my mum offer to lend him her phone to call the police. She wasn't very pleased and started muttering something about needing bleach for when he gave it back.

He seemed to be taking ages on the phone, which was when I realised that he had moved on from speaking to the police and was now having a row with his boss. I was trying not to get too close (in case I fell in the fish), but I could hear him saying, *'I told you months ago that those back doors were dodgy,'* followed by, *'They're starting to thaw out – there's no way I can get them to France now.'*

I looked round, and my mum had disappeared. I spotted a mini supermarket across the road. So that was that mystery solved. She'd been looking for an excuse to replace the baguette we forgot for the last five hours.

6.03 p.m.

My mum came out of the supermarket *(after 19 whole minutes — what on earth was she doing in there?)* with the French bread and a pack of 40 anti-bacterial wipes. She used all of them to clean her phone.

By the time we got back in the car, I didn't smell good. Troy had unpacked his deodorant from his bag in preparation. He sprayed me. And then he sprayed his hair *(to prevent the absorption).*

When Troy's Lynx Africa deodorant fog had cleared, my dad started to reverse out of the traffic jam which was now being cleared by the police. He turned round to check through the back window that he wasn't going to hit anything *(like maybe a ticket barrier . . . for example)*, took one look at me and his face went white. Then he started to scream. **REALLY LOUDLY**. Then he started to try to throw himself out of the car.

In his panic, Dad didn't seem able to unbuckle his seat belt, so he was trapped. Until my mum set him free and then he just fell out of the door on to the pavement.

I really had no idea what was going on with him
(which is not unusual). Until I looked down at my
shoulder.

And there it was.

A fish eye.

And judging by the slime dripping out
from it, I think it might have **popped** in the heat.

6.15 p.m. – That Ship Has Sailed

By the time we got to the port, our ferry was already
halfway to France.

As we approached the entrance, Dad declared, 'Don't worry, guys. I've got this.'

Which meant this was likely to be a disaster.

'Hello, sir,' he said without looking up at the booth.

It was a bad start.

'My name's Jane,' the person in the booth replied with her teeth gritted. 'How can I help?' She was clearly in no mood to be helpful.

'Well, the thing is . . .' my dad continued. 'It hasn't been plain sailing, so we've missed the boat.'

Oh. My. GOD. This was terrible. He was going to need a lot more than sea-based clichés to get Jane onside.

But then it got worse *(if that was even possible)*. Dad started to explain the lorry delay.

'You see, the fish were all over the PLAICE and we just couldn't move. It was an act of COD.'

He ploughed on.

Jane stopped listening.

'Next availability is the ten thirty-seven a.m.

crossing tomorrow morning,' said Jane, cutting my dad off midway through saying something about a *'feeling in his SOLE'.*

Seriously?

There must be something available before then. I'd rather try to swim to France than spend a whole night at the port listening to my dad's fish jokes and eating tins of bouillabaisse again.

'Dad, move the car up and let me speak to her,' I said from behind his seat. After the fish-eye incident he'd made me and Troy swap places so I wasn't in his eyeline.

I wound down the window.

'Excuse me,' I said. *'Can we take a space if there has been a cancellation?'*

The mackerel lorry was surely a cancellation?

'There haven't been any,' said Jane without even checking. She even laughed slightly, which made me think that Jane was enjoying our problems a little too much.

'Can you double check?' I pleaded. *'The cancellation would be from HOOK, LINE AND SINKER FISH TRANSPORTATION.'*

(I think that was the name on the side of the lorry.)
'They are **definitely** *not going to France today.'*

Jane looked as if she had swallowed a wasp when she glanced up from her computer.

'Hmmm. Looks like they just called. There's a space on the seven forty-two p.m.'

That was only 52 minutes from now. **YES. YES. YES.**

'Move on through, please,' spat Jane, practically throwing the new ticket through the car window.

'Thanks. You have a **WHALE** *of a time with the rest of your day,'* shouted my dad as we drove off.

Seriously?

He **REALLY** needs to learn to quit while he is ahead . . .

7.00 p.m.

We are now waiting in the queue for the 7.42 p.m. ferry and my mum is handing round the bag of bonbons to *'keep us going'*. Going until when? I have no idea, but I have a bad feeling that she means . . . until we have a chance to crack open the tins. So I am going to eat as many bonbons as I possibly can.

I am feeling quite happy. I think I did pretty well to get us on this ferry. But no one else has even mentioned this. Although to be fair, no one has mentioned much since the bonbons appeared.

Anyway, it has got me thinking, because . . . I have been wondering lately whether **this** might be my **thing**. The **thing** that I am good at.

You see, for about a gazillion years Priya has been singing and playing the guitar. It is her **thing**. She is **amazing**. Everyone says she should go on *Britain's Got Talent*. But she won't try because she is still embarrassed that she thought Ant & Dec was **one** person. *First name:* **Anton**, *surname:* **Dec**.

And Edward is **determined** to be a doctor. He has it all mapped out in a notebook he has called *'The Plan'*. Maisie wants to be a **movie star**. She says she's already a professional actress anyway. The AA told Priya that Maisie was paid to be in an advert for teabags. The weird thing is that I have seen it — the advert. And I definitely didn't see Maisie in it. Unless she was dressed up as a farmer the same age as my grandad. So maybe being paid for it and actually being on the TV are not the same thing . . . **Was she backstage?** I'm still confused on that one.

Troy doesn't need a **thing**. He has his **hair** and his never-ending queue of **adoring fans**, so he'll be fine whatever happens *(head-scream)*.

Even Douglas Joiner has a **thing**. He is really good with computers. He showed Mrs Travers how to link up her mobile phone to her doorbell a few weeks ago. Now she can answer the door when she isn't in. According to Douglas, Mrs Travers thought this was **amazing**. But it sounded like a terrible idea to me . . . **why would you want to open your front door when you are 12 miles away teaching an English lesson? Unless you really want to get all your stuff stolen . . .?**

Anyway, I need a **thing**. Something that *I* am good at. I want someone *(anyone)* to say, 'Harper Drew . . . *she's the one that's BRILLIANT at . . .'* And until now, there hasn't been a whole load of obvious endings to that sentence. It's definitely not singing – I got asked to mime in the end-of-term performance because I was making the whole class sound out of tune. And it might not be netball – my team lost the house final when I forgot we'd switched ends at half-time and scored a really great goal . . . for the other team.

So I was drawing a big fat nothing on this **'thing'** **thing**.

Until now. Because I'm thinking that maybe MAKING STUFF HAPPEN could be my **thing**. FIXING SITUATIONS and even making some money on the side too.

Today is a good example. But there is other stuff too. The fundraising for the stairlift is going well so far. I have organised everything and raised most of the money. There have been lemonade, cake and toy stalls. And if you can sponsor it . . . then we have tried it. I even donated half a metre of my hair to a wig charity and raised £400. I still regret not being able to convince Troy to join in on that one. With the amount of hair he has I thought we could hit the stairlift target in one go. But he said he couldn't spare a single strand because every **ONE** was **VITAL** to his **'LOOK'**.

The only disaster we had was when I organised the pet **hamster** race. There were too many entries and we lost control of the starting line. There were **hamsters** all over the place. And Daniel Muldoon's took a wrong turn up Mrs Travers's leg. I have never seen anyone **SCREAM** so **LOUD** or **RUN** so **FAST** . . . and that was just the **hamster**.

But, my **BIGGEST** win was convincing my mum's boss to get the supermarket to match all of our donations. I think he thought we had only raised a few pounds, so when I told him that we had reached £2,000, he said he would have to ask the fresh produce and the drinks departments to chip in too. Which they did.

So, we are at £4,153 now. And I have made all the arrangements for the **BIG** event – the one I am counting on to get us close to the target of £5,500. The

major car boot sale in town at the end of the holidays.
I can't wait. I LOVE **(LOVE LOVE)** a car boot sale.

Then there is the *(still secret from my mum)* fixing that
I did last year when my dad needed some urgent
assistance. He had **accidentally** ordered a **hundred**
phone cases on the internet . . . instead of **one** *(he leant
his elbow on the zero button by mistake).*

They arrived all the way from China. The **good** news
was that he had only bought cheap ones. The **bad** news
was that they couldn't be returned. My dad hid the extra
cases from my mum. But I found them because he was in a
hurry and stashed them under my bed thinking he didn't
have time to get the ladder and put them up in the loft. It
did make me wonder what else he might have stashed in
the loft though.

Anyway, after about a week of worrying Mum might
look under my bed, I had a brainwave. There was a shop
right by school called *We Buy Any Phone.* I got my dad to
drop me there early one Wednesday and I asked them
whether the *'We Buy Any . . .'* might extend to phone

cases too. The answer was **YES**. They offered me 75p per case. **No way** was I going to take that though. It was like they thought I was too young to be selling a high-quality item. I wasn't selling a high-quality item. But they didn't need to know that. So I did that trick of walking away and saying I had someone else interested (*Troy says this works every time . . . although it didn't on Troyz Beanz*). They instantly offered £1.50 a case. And after a lengthy inspection of each one (*all 99 of them, I was really late for school*), the deal was done.

Dad made me give him £1 per case, which I thought was steep given that I had really got him out of a big hole with my mum. And I kept the rest: £49.50. This was before we needed the money for the stairlift so I bought some of those skate shoes with wheels in them. Maisie Felix had a pair and I had wanted some for about a year.

So . . . yes . . . maybe this . . . FIXING SITUATIONS . . . is going to be **my thing**.

If it is, I can't have inherited it from my dad. After the phone cases, the missed ferry and the ticket-barrier crash incident, *CREATING* SITUATIONS is clearly **HIS thing**.

7 August

THE JOURNEY

PART TWO

6 a.m.

We've arrived. Well, we haven't **quite** arrived. We are waiting in the car park of a French supermarket for it to open at 7 a.m. We can't get the key to the house until 2 p.m., so where better to wait than a *hypermarché* the size of **14** football pitches?

The journey timings for our holidays are always a mystery. They are either perfectly timed if you want to spend six hours in a French supermarket. Or a **DISASTER** if you don't. Guess the family are split on that one? My mum thinks it is one of the best parts of the holiday.

We've been in the car for almost **16** hours. If you don't count:

90 minutes on the ferry. I felt so seasick I had to lie face down on the top deck the whole way.

SEVEN stops for the toilet.

ONE stop to change the Prune's trousers after he had an accident before we had an eighth toilet stop.

45 minutes in a layby somewhere south of Calais while we ate some baguettes for dinner *(brought with us from England)*.

The thing is, the trip doesn't need to take this long. **BUT** my mum and dad refuse to use the motorway. In France you have to pay to use the bigger, better, **QUICKER** roads. And now that we are back to saving up again for the new downstairs carpet *(and let's not even mention the minibus window)* there was a whole €73.50 to be saved if we used something called the **N** roads.

ℕ must stand for ℕOT **VERY GOOD**. Or maybe for ℕOWHERE **NEAR AS GOOD AS THE MOTORWAY.** Because the ℕ roads are really narrow, really twisty and really dark. And the chances of getting stuck behind a tractor going at one mile per hour are very high. Which means that the chances of my dad deciding to risk an overtake manoeuvre that should only happen on a Formula 1 racing track are also very high. The journey was a **DANGEROUS** business.

I do get that €73.50 is quite a lot of money. It probably buys quite a lot of downstairs carpet. But this meant an extra FOUR **HOURS** in the car. An extra FOUR **HOURS** where it was quite likely that my dad might swerve round a horsebox and plunge us all into a ditch. **I am not sure these N roads are the right decision.**

No one really got any sleep either. **Except my mum**. When she wasn't driving, she was in the passenger seat **SNORING**. In biology we did a project on some monkeys that snore so **loudly** you can hear

them from three miles away.
I think they can
probably hear
my mum on
the International
Space Station.

I tried to use my
mega-noise-reducing headphones that I'd
got last Christmas. But they **ran out** of battery after
about **FOUR** minutes. I think they couldn't cope with
the effort that was needed to drown out the snoring.

Troy **wouldn't** put his head on his pillow in case it
ruined his **hair** permanently. So he spent the night in
the car trying to keep himself awake by *'working on his
skateboard'*. I was pretty mad that he had been
allowed to bring the skateboard in the car in the first
place. But my mum had said he could because *'the
skateboard is very important to Troy right now'*.

'Edward is very important to me, can I bring him?'
I had tried to argue.

'Don't be ridiculous, Harper,' came the reply from Mum as she carried Troy's bag and the skateboard into the car for him.

Troy was **CLICKING** and **FLICKING** around with a  spanner until about 3 a.m. **At one point** he even got out a bottle of something that SMELLED very much like petrol and started greasing the two wheels. Mum didn't notice because she was **snoring** and Dad says he has **no sense of smell** (which, if true, is a very good thing on this car journey).

Eventually Troy ran out of things to UNSCREW on the skateboard and fell asleep on it. When we arrived at the *hypermarché* car park he woke up with the imprint of one of the wheels across his forehead.

And ... **HIS HAIR IS TOTALLY FLAT**.

7 a.m.

I had to stop writing for a bit. Troy was out of the car stretching his legs when he saw his hair in the car's wing mirror. I thought he **might actually collapse**. But he seemed to recover and started to sprint to the *hypermarché* entrance screaming something about dry shampoo and whether or not it had been invented yet in France.

This was all the excuse my mum needed. We were standing in the **salami aisle** within **30 seconds**. We could see *(and hear)* Troy talking to an extremely confused-looking shop assistant. Troy was pointing to his head and shouting, '**CHEVAL! CHEVAL! CHEVAL!**' *Cheval* **means horse**.

If he'd put anything more than ZERO effort into French class, Troy might have known the word for hair **(cheveux)**.

We spent **two hours** inside the *hypermarché*. Which is a long time in a French supermarket when you have a car so full of French food already that you

88

could open your own rival shop. **One whole hour**
was spent in the **pens aisle**. My mum thinks that
they sell the best pens in France. *'Harper, if* **un** *pen
has enough ink for* **cinq** *hours of writing, how many
days will the pen last if I write* **vingt** *words per
minute for* **soixante** *minutes each day?'* The maths
questions are always a whole new shape of nightmare
on holiday because Mum insists on saying the numbers
in French. The clicky finger thing went on a long time
while I tried to decode this one.

Anyway, in the end we came out with **13 permanent
markers, a fountain pen** and most of the **hair product
aisle**. My dad spent **€37** on fixing up Troy's head.

Is it just me? . . . but that is half the saving of
not going on the motorway! We could have had two
hours less in the car. Or two metres of downstairs
carpet. But this is the effect Troy has on my parents

. . . they do whatever he wants.

On the way out, I noticed that a film set was being set up outside the entrance. It looked like a mini festival. There were sparkly lights, little blue and pink tepee tents and fake grass. And what appeared to be a dozen or so tins of beans stacked in a way that made them look like a campfire.

We decided they must be getting ready to make an advert. Troy declared they might want his help *'after the success of Troyz Beanz'*. He was completely serious. I couldn't help but laugh.

'Not if they actually want to sell any they won't,' I replied. My mum told me not to be mean to Troy.

Something about the set made my **teeth itch**. It was making me think of Maisie and her camping party. Minus the beans of course. Maisie wouldn't have beans at the festival – not after the sleeping bag incident last time, let's be honest.

And that was when I had THE IDEA.

Of exactly how to make sure I get invited . . .

10 a.m. – The Master Plan

GET UNCLE PAUL THE MOVIE PRODUCER
TO MAKE A TV SHOW OUT OF MAISIE'S PARTY.

★ ★ ★ ★ ★ ★ ★ ★ ★ ★

Like a reality show. With Maisie as the star.

Maisie Felix LOVES to be the centre of attention.
If I can make that happen, then there is sure to be an
invite with my name on it. This could be huge. After all,
Maisie wants to be famous and she already thinks she is
an actress after that teabag advert she says she was in.
This could be the start of her path to global stardom.
And I could be the one to make it happen.

We could have a **PREMIERE**. Maisie has a massive TV
at her house. It is **bigger** than the screen at the local
cinema and I bet she would love to have **EVERYONE** over
to watch her starring in her own show. Uncle Paul could
lend us his red carpet. He got it from OnlineCarpets and
so far he hasn't had much use for it. Except he did get it
out in the garden once to practise his 'walk' for the
Oscars (he wasn't even going to the Oscars).

Is it just me? But surely if you are a real movie producer, you don't need to bring your own red carpet. That gets provided by someone else, right? You don't have to bring it in the boot of your own car and then lay it yourself outside the Odeon in Leicester Square?

Anyway, I haven't got time to think about that right now. I need to put this plan into action.

12 noon

In the car on the way to the gite, I asked my mum if I could call Uncle Paul and ask him.

She was in a good mood. Fresh out of the supermarket. She said she would let me call Paul.

But Troy was now being **EXTRA** irritating. He had made up a song and taught it to the Prune. And they were both singing very loudly. **On repeat**. Even my dad joined in for one verse.

'Maisie, Maisie, give her your answer do,
Harper's going crazy all for an invite from you,
She's desperate to go to your festival,
But she's as boring as a vegetable,
So she's going to call, and bribe Uncle Paul,
She's a seriously uncool Drew.'

I could barely hear Uncle Paul with all the singing in the back seat, but he was acting very weird. He didn't stay on the phone long. He said he was in the middle of auditioning stunt doubles and didn't have much time. But I thought I could hear a supermarket tannoy in the background saying, 'Help needed on aisle five,' and when I hung up, he definitely asked me if I needed a carrier bag. Why would he say that? Unless he was working at a supermarket?

'Maybe his next film takes place on a checkout at the local shop?' said Troy when I mentioned it. At least he had stopped with the singing.

'I should have been asked to audition for that. I would make a brilliant stunt double,' my dad said grumpily while flexing his arm muscles and making a fist. 'I look exactly like that guy who plays Spider-Man from behind.'

'From behind what?' laughed Troy. 'From behind a tree on a really dark night?'

And then, trying to impress Troy (I think), my dad did his best impression of a Spider-Man punch. But he cracked his fist on the car windscreen. And now he thinks he's broken his thumb.

But the main thing is: Uncle Paul agreed to make the Maisie movie.

YEESSSS!

2 p.m. - Llama Glama Drama

We arrived at the gite just after two o'clock. The key to the front door was in a small safe attached to the wall of the house. Dad opened it and immediately managed to fumble and **drop the key** down the nearest drain.

We had only been there **30 seconds**, and we were locked out.

WELCOME TO THE DREW FAMILY HOLIDAY *(head-scream)*. 9.5/10 ON THE DREW DIAL.

I wanted to ask Mum if I could text Maisie with the plan for a party invite, but the Prune was having a **meltdown** because he wanted to go in the pool. He was hysterical so I didn't dare break it to him that there was **no pool**. Mum picked the Prune up and started muttering something about cleaning under her breath. She had her bleach out of the car boot, all ready for the cleaning session that has to take place at the start of all holidays. Now she was going to have to wait.

She wasn't happy.

This probably wasn't the right moment to text Maisie.

My dad ran next door and, for once, he was in luck. The guy next door is called Derek and is from Stockport, which isn't quite what we were expecting. He had a spare key. He also has **two pet llamas,** which was even more of a surprise. Especially when he brought them both with him to open our gite.

'Follow me, guys. You on holiday?' asked Derek.

'No,' said my dad. 'I play football for Paris Saint-Germain and I think I took a wrong turn on the way to training.' Dad almost doubled over laughing at his own joke.

'I don't think you'll make the first team, mate,' replied Derek, also laughing. 'You'd raise the average age of the whole team by about twenty years.'

My dad did **NOT** look happy. But at the mention of averages, my mum's fixation on the cleaning seemed to get less severe. Her mood always improves when she senses an opportunity for a maths question. I knew she was about to ask me to work out the age of the rest of the team.

But before she could say anything, Dad got there first.

'Do you have the key then?' he said. He was clearly

offended by Derek's joke about his age. And clearly no longer in any mood to make friends, because he followed up with, 'What on earth are THEY doing here?'

My dad pointed to the two llamas. One of them was now weeing on the wheel of our car. 'This is Ester – and that's Fester over there cleaning your tyres.'
I thought my mum was going to pass out at Derek's definition of 'cleaning'.

'They're brother and sister, just like you two,' he carried on, nodding towards me and Troy, who was not happy that his hair had just been compared to that of an incontinent llama. 'They make lovely silky jumpers. We have a market stall. Saturdays at nine a.m.' explained Derek as if that was the answer to Dad's question. 'They did have another brother, Leicester, but we sadly lost him to Berserk Llama Syndrome.'

'What is Berserk Llama Syndrome?' I asked.

Now there was a string of words I never thought I would say.

But then. Out of nowhere. As if this gite doorstep chit-chat couldn't get any weirder . . .

TROY chips in. 'Yeah, Berserk Llama Syndrome is really terrible. We learnt about it in geography.'

Mum and Dad stared at Troy with pride. Like he was David Attenborough all of a sudden.

'Yeah, they like just get cuddled too much when they are babies and then . . . they go berserk . . .' Troy trailed off. (I got Mum to google it later: Berserk Llama Syndrome. Annoyingly Troy was right.)

Derek looked as if he might cry, and attempted to cover Ester's huge ears, as if the memory was still too raw.

This made me laugh. Suddenly it all made sense . . . If getting hugged too much when they are young makes llamas go **BERSERK** when they are older, it isn't surprising that Troy's **DREW DIAL RATING** is so high. With the level of adoration my parents have for Troy, he must have been the most cuddled child in history.

Berserk Troy Syndrome – watch this space . . .

Dad had finally had enough. And he looked like he might be about to keel over with tiredness. Mum finally took the keys from Derek and we headed inside the gite.

'Watch out for the bats,' Derek shouted after us as he, Ester and Fester (but not Leicester) sloped back next door.

Sorry, what?

'Bats?' shouted Troy. 'Is there a table tennis table?' But Derek and the llamas were long gone. Something tells me the bats Derek was warning us about **AREN'T** the table tennis kind.

5 p.m.

As usual, the gite is **not quite as nice** as my mum had hoped it would be. This happens every year.

She books the holiday and then builds it up, so that by the time we arrive, the **small cottage** on the outskirts of nowhere has magically turned into a **five-star luxury resort** with a pool and a personal waiter ready to serve her drinks *(or bleach)* day or night.

Seriously, though, last year we were **MISSING** an **inside toilet**. And since there was only supposed to be **ONE** inside toilet, this meant there was **NO inside toilet**. So we all had to use an **outside Portaloo**. Which was not ideal during the day, and a whole world of problems at night.

This year, according to Mum, there are several issues. The rooms look **smaller** than they did in the pictures, the kitchen doesn't seem to have a sink and there is a bedroom **MISSING**, which worryingly means we don't have enough beds.

But there is a **massive** garden which has a trampoline in it, so me and the Prune are very happy.

While Mum was busy going in and out of the rooms, and Dad had a snooze on the sofa, we had great fun.

The Prune loves to sit down while I jump up and down like a wild salmon. It makes him bounce around all over the place and he laughs like he might never stop. Troy would only watch – apparently he 'might get a static shock from the metal frame', which would make his hair frizzy. His loss.

Then we did **THE CLEAN**.

And my mum's mood really improved. It's her **second** favourite part of the holiday *(after a visit to the hypermarché pens aisle)* – her bleaching of the entire house before anyone touches anything. We all know what we have to do:

1. My mum locates any cleaning cloths and dishcloths, puts them in a saucepan and **boils** them. Even if they are **new** out of the packet.

She says you can't be **too careful**.

2. My dad bleaches the bathroom and is responsible for **'surfaces'**, although he has never been quite clear of the definition of **'surfaces'**, and last year he **bleached the curtains**. They went a shade of light orange and we had to buy new ones (another trip to the hypermarché).

3. I mop the floors. With **bleach**. After the mop has been **dunked** in the **boiling saucepan** of dishcloths.

4. Troy is **supposed** to bleach the kitchen

sink, but this time, there **isn't** a sink. He went to lie down on the sofa thinking he had lucked out, until my mum sent him outside to bleach the wheel of the car that Fester had weed on.

5. The Prune is lucky. He is still **'too young for the clean'.**

7 p.m.

By the time we finished it was getting dark. My dad unpacked the car and my mum was about to put away all the French food we had brought with us. She loves this bit too. And always asks me to calculate the bulk saving we have made on all the tins as she admires them stacked on top of each other in the cupboard.

That was when we found the missing bedroom.

What looks like a door to a cupboard in the kitchen is in fact the entrance to a small room with two single beds in it. It has a really high ceiling. And we could hear a **strange** amount of **squeaking** coming from above.

When we looked up at the ceiling it was **black**.
And it was **moving**.

The bats.

All of the bats. **ACTUAL
BATS.** *A colony.* *Flying.*
In and out of a window in the
roof, which was wide open.

Derek had *definitely* not
meant table tennis bats.

My mum SCREAMED. She
picked up the Prune to
protect herself. We all ran
for it – well almost all of us.

Troy slammed the door shut. leaving my dad in there.

*'Don't open that door, Troy. Just leave him in
there!'* shouted my mum. She was pointing a bottle of
bleach at the door like it was an automatic weapon.

'let me out NOW, Eve!' screamed my dad at my

mum, scratching at the other side of the door. *'Do they bite, Troy? Oh god. Troy, do they bite? Tell me NOW – do they bite?'*

My dad obviously thinks that Troy's animal knowledge isn't just limited to berserk llamas and includes the life and times of the bat too.

But it doesn't.

'No clue, Dad.' Troy shrugged and *(as if the family panic was just too much effort)* he left to lie on the sofa.

'I think I can feel one on me. ON MY NECK. Oh goooooooodddddddd!' shouted Dad. The pulling at the door handle was getting louder and more frantic. He obviously didn't realise he could just turn it and escape now that **Troy was long gone**.

'Dad, calm down,' I said. *'They only bite if they are provoked.'*

Just after I said that, there was a gut-wrenching **HOWL** and a **MASSIVE** CRASH. Dad had pulled the door off its hinges and was lying underneath it on the floor of the bat bedroom.

And now he thinks he has broken his other thumb.

8 p.m. – It's Buzzing

With no door to the bat cave (as Troy is now calling it), the bats have taken full advantage of our (very clean) holiday home.

Only my mum and dad's bedroom is bat-less. Mum managed to barricade herself inside while my Dad was still lying underneath the door to the bat cave. She isn't coming out. Nor is her phone, so I can't even text Maisie. And at the moment, she isn't letting **anyone** else in.

My dad grabbed a tin of chicken chasseur and he's now sitting on the trampoline with Troy and the Prune. From the window, I can see Troy opening the tin (because of my dad's current thumb problems).

That is one French meal I am definitely staying out of, so I'm braving the sofa with three leftover bonbons. The bats are everywhere. Clicking away overhead. If I close my eyes (which I won't in case one lands on me), they sound a lot like my mum when she asks a maths question and her finger clicking goes wild.

This is all bringing back the memory of the time Mr Ejiofor found a beehive behind the art-room display wall at school.

We could all hear the buzzing. Edward didn't want to sit anywhere near, so I swapped places with him and was right underneath it.

'Sir, that display wall is buzzing,' Edward had been telling Mr Ejiofor for weeks.

'I know, Edward,' was the reply that kept coming from Mr Ejiofor. *'That is the power of art. It creates a buzz where there was no buzz.'*

'But, sir.' Edward didn't let it go. Once he is convinced of something, Edward is always pretty determined. *'It sounds like something is alive in there.'*

'I know, Edward,' said Mr Ejiofor again. *'That is the power of art. It brings the still to life.'*

I loved Edward's persistence, but he was getting **nowhere**. Which wasn't surprising. Mr Ejiofor was quite often in his own world. He sometimes came into class with his ear bandaged up because he said he felt 'closer to Vincent van Gogh' that way.

Mr Ejiofor came back to the real world pretty quickly after he tried to add Douglas Joiner's collage of *The Sunflowers* to the wall display. There was so much glue on the picture that Mr Ejiofor's staple gun wouldn't work and he borrowed a hammer and some nails from Mr Longden in design and tech. He went a bit too hard with the first nail and knocked a hole in the wall.

Which was when we discovered the beehive.

When the beekeepers arrived, they said there were **SIXTY THOUSAND** bees in there. **FIVE** of them came to a sticky end on Douglas Joiner's sunflowers. And **ONE** stung Mr Ejiofor. **On his ear**. Which I think he was secretly pleased about because it gave him an excuse to wear his bandage for the following three months.

Is it just me? But I did feel for that bee . . . Having lived for ages inside the wall in the school art room, it finally made its bid for freedom and then died within 30 seconds after a **COLLISION** with an earlobe. Not ideal.

Anyway, the remaining **59,994 BEES** swarmed the art-room ceiling, requiring a mass evacuation. And the school had to close for the rest of the day.

Douglas Joiner was *(for that afternoon at least)* the most popular kid in school. Maisie was **furious**.

Things went back to normal the next morning though. When he turned up with six slices of toast in his PE bag.

'In case there is loads of spare honey,' he said.

8 August

BACK IN THE CAR

6 a.m.

That was possibly the worst night's sleep I have **EVER** had.

My mum took some persuading that it was the right thing to do to let the rest of us into the bat-free bedroom. I had to promise to bring the bleach *(just in case)* and we all had to climb in through the window.

The problem was that there was **only one bed**. And there were **five** of us.

Troy slept in the **bath** in the **en-suite bathroom**. It made sense. He'd already be in the right place ready to start on his hair the minute he woke up.

The Prune slept in the **bottom drawer** of the **wardrobe**. It was just long enough for him if he didn't stretch his legs out.

Me and my mum and my dad all slept in the **bed**. I was quite pleased about this to start with.

I was **wrong**. I got **zero** sleep.

My mum snored almost all night. It was so LOUD that in the end my dad held her nostrils shut. But to be able to reach over to do that he had to rest his elbow on my cheekbone. It is hard to sleep with a bony elbow digging in to your face.

Just as I was finally falling asleep, my dad got up to use the toilet and **forgot** that Troy was asleep in the bath . . . until he turned the light on. While he was making a hasty exit, my dad **accidentally knocked** the Prune's **drawer shut**.

That was it. The Prune was in a frenzy until the sun came up. I couldn't really blame him. He was basically terrified. He'd had a narrow escape from the bats, only to be shut in a sock drawer for a good minute until Dad realised his mistake.

It is now 6.30 a.m. And we are back in the supermarket car park. Waiting for it to open. **Again.**

9 a.m. – Rap Lessons

We are going home. My mum is in tears. Which is the only time I have ever seen her cry within 100 metres of a supermarket. I feel really sorry for her. She loves the French holiday. And ours appears to be over. After one day. **A DREW FAMILY RECORD.**

There was a call to the gite owner to see if she might do something about the bats. But bats are a protected species and the gite owner said she was sorry, but if she had to choose between us or the bats, she wasn't choosing us. And she wasn't giving us our money back either. Something about the small print and *'guests needing to be tolerant of local wildlife'.* And the damage my dad had done to the door of the bat cave didn't help our case.

Derek said we could stay next door with him. But he only has two bedrooms, which would have meant me, Troy and the Prune camping in his garden. With the llamas and more bats probably. **NO WAY. NO WAY. NO WAY** was I doing that.

Derek turned out to be pretty cool in the end.

He helped us to load the car back up and gave the Prune a ride on Ester and Fester. My mum gave him four tins of beef bourguignon and a bottle of bleach to say thank you.

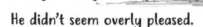

He didn't seem overly pleased.

My dad has promised that after we have cheered my mum up with one last trip to the **cheese aisle** we will stop at the lake for the day before we drive back. I **really** want to do the lilo loafing and I think Dad does too. After all, he has been doing his secret-not-so-secret training for a whole year at the local swimming pool.

I also **need** to text Maisie.

This is why I need my **own** phone. I can't keep relying on my mum.

And it is embarrassing. Maisie has a brand-new phone

— as she was so keen to tell me when I was basically glued to the pavement outside her house. She even has a specially made gold case which says 'Maisie Might Call (If You're Lucky)'.

Even Priya has got a phone. Her dad gave her his old one. But he forgot to delete his old messages and Priya found out that he had been having **secret lessons** in **how to rap**. Priya's dad doesn't look very much like a rapper. He works for the council as an accountant. But she says she was a bit relieved about the messages. She had caught him twice shouting into the bathroom mirror. Something about *'busting with my crew'*. At least that makes sense now, she says.

I am not sure it makes any sense. **WHY** was her dad taking **RAP** lessons? Surely they aren't normally top of a dad's list of hobbies? Maybe mayhem is catching and living next door to the Drew family for the last 10 years had affected him.

But anyway. I **NEED** to text Maisie. I **NEED** my own phone.

10 a.m. - The Lake

We are at the lake. But we are nowhere near the lake. We are on the grass in the car park.

This could only be happening to the Drew family.

The lake costs €15 per adult and €8 per child to go swimming. But it is free from 4 p.m. *(when it must go dark or the lake gets infested with piranhas or something)*.

So guess what? *'In the interests of the downstairs carpet,'* *(according to my dad)* we are waiting until 4 p.m. so we can save the €46 entrance fee *(the Prune goes free – I didn't get the maths wrong, Mum . . . in case you are reading this)*.

It is currently 10 a.m.

Seriously?

Dad's **DREW DIAL RATING** has just gone up. To **9.9999/10**. It is **SIX WHOLE HOURS** until 4 p.m.

My mum seems to think this wait is a good idea too. She is asleep *(and snoring)* on the grass. Troy is at the other side of the car park on his phone, taking pictures of his hairstyle for his skateboarding vlog. Apparently the wind is better for his hair over there.

My dad decided we should play a game to pass the time, which he called **CAR BOOT DROP**. My grandad invented this one apparently. And so Dad is calling it *'Drew family history'* – which is worrying if this is the best legacy we have. Because it involves climbing on to the roof of the car and then using the back windscreen to slide down. It is one of the least safe games I have ever seen Dad invent. It didn't start well either. He went first and ripped the windscreen wiper off the back window with his bottom.

That was going to cost more than €46 to fix right there.

Seriously?

But with the wiper gone, **CAR BOOT DROP** was pretty fun. We were not going to be able to do it for six whole hours though.

And after a while I realised that Dad wasn't even playing any more and was asleep on the grass next to my mum.

I need to do something. For a start I can hear all the kids splashing around in the lake, which is driving me a bit *(a lot)* crazy. And I am not sure how but the Prune is already wearing his swim shorts.

WE CAN'T WAIT ANY LONGER.

11.30 a.m.

I opened the boot of the car to see what I could find. I wondered if I could sell Troy's skateboard to anyone arriving in the car park for €46. But I decided against that because:

⇨

1. *It only had two wheels, so I couldn't see anyone actually giving me money for it.*

2. *Mum and Dad **seemed to believe** that Troy would make millions from this vlog thing, so they'd probably be **really annoyed** with me.*

3. Maybe *I couldn't do that to Troy. But that was only a maybe . . .*

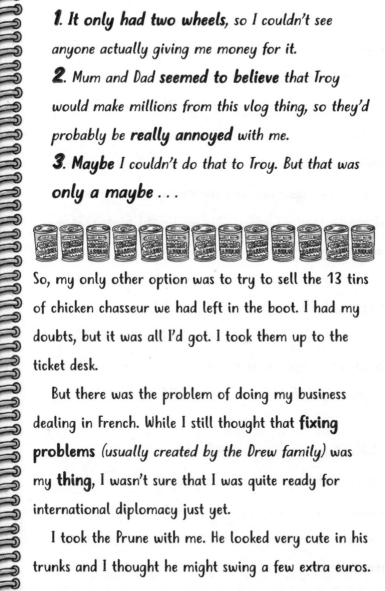

So, my only other option was to try to sell the 13 tins of chicken chasseur we had left in the boot. I had my doubts, but it was all I'd got. I took them up to the ticket desk.

But there was the problem of doing my business dealing in French. While I still thought that **fixing problems** (usually created by the Drew family) was my **thing**, I wasn't sure that I was quite ready for international diplomacy just yet.

I took the Prune with me. He looked very cute in his trunks and I thought he might swing a few extra euros.

I was putting the tins on the counter and gearing up my best French when the ticket woman said, *'You're a waiter, aren't you?'*

She was English. Which was good news.

'What does that mean?' I asked.

'You're waiting. You're Waiters.' She rolled her eyes and sighed. *'Your parents are trying to save the entrance fee by making you wait until four o'clock, aren't they?'*

She was also quite grumpy. Bad news. Maybe she didn't want the tins of chicken.

The fact that there was a name for us, **'WAITERS'**, actually made me quite happy. It must have meant that other people apart from the Drew family did things like this.

'Do lots of people do this then?' I asked.

'Only if they're fools,' she said, half laughing.

Well, that made more sense.

'The sign on the way in clearly says that the lake shuts at four thirty p.m. By the time you get down

there and get changed you'll barely have got your hair wet and you'll have to come out.'

That would suit Troy. But it really did mean I needed to get us in now.

I went in big on the chicken chasseur. Told her how tasty it was *(it really isn't)* and that it cost £3.50 a tin usually so it really was a good deal if she could just see her way to letting us in. Nowish.

'Why would I want those?' she said. 'I live in France. I didn't even buy those when I lived in Stockport.'

I mean . . . she had a point. But why was everyone round here from Stockport in England?

I was getting nowhere.

Until out of the blue she said, 'Now, if you had a bottle of Domestos, THEN I'd be interested. French bleach just isn't the same. It's all runny and . . .'

Oh my goodness. This was the only time that my mum's cleaning obsession had **EVER** been a good thing. I left the ticket seller listing the problems with French bleach . . . and she was still going when I got

121

back with the three bottles we had in the boot.

'It doesn't even smell that fresh, and it really stains if you spill it . . . WOW!' she shouted when she saw what I was carrying. 'How many tickets do you want?'

We were IN. She even threw in four free goes on the waterslide.

12 noon

Before I woke my mum and dad with the good news that I had saved us five hours of complete and utter boredom, I decided to borrow my mum's phone and text Maisie.

Hi Maisie. It is Harper here

I wondered if I needed to say Harper Drew? Would she know it was from me? Cringe . . . If I had my own phone none of this would be a problem.

> How are the party plans?

That sounded breezy.

Did it sound breezy? Or a bit too keen?

> Just wondered if you wanted to record the event? My uncle Paul is a Hollywood movie producer. He could make a show of the party and we could have a premiere after? XXX

Kisses or an emoji? Not sure . . .

SEND. It had gone. TEETH ITCHING!

A message came straight back.

> Is this Harper Johnson, Harper Rai-Jaswal or Harper Drew?

Nightmare. I wasn't even the first Harper she thought of.

And then another message:

PS It is a festival not a party

Seriously? This was really hard work.

It is Harper Drew. I'm borrowing my
mum's phone because mine's broken ☹

Not true. I don't have a phone, which she knows. I gave
her Priya's number last time, which she also knows. BUT I
was trying to style it out.
   And then . . .

♥ the movie idea. We can have the premiere
at my house after the festival. Come early to
the festival too. You can help decorate. M x

Great. I'll need to bring Priya as well. H x

I thought I would sort this out while I was on a roll
with Maisie.

> No problem, Princess. Tell her
> no cola bottles though. M x

She just couldn't resist.

But . . . my teeth have just stopped itching.

3 p.m.
BREAKING NEWS:

Troy just fell in the lake.

Head first from an
inflatable pink flamingo.

And his hair is all over
the place.

And there is nowhere to
plug in the hairdryer.

And it is a crisis.

And Mum and Dad have just actually offered to
blow on his head to imitate a hairdryer while he
styles it.

And . . . I am not sure what else to say right now.

3.45 p.m.

Now we're back in the car, I thought I would explain . . . It all started when my dad ran to the lake with the lilo under his arm. He looked like he had been born ready for this moment.

My dad had made it to a kneel, like last year, but it looked as if he was much steadier this time. Yes, he was gearing up for the final manoeuvre up to his feet, smiling wildly, waving at my mum . . . and then the lilo **EXPLODED**. And my dad sank – straight down with the lilo folding around him like a sandwich on both sides. It was like watching a giant sinking hotdog.

The lifeguard got very excited. I can only think that he hadn't had anything to do for a few days because he mounted a rescue mission that would have been more appropriate for a national emergency than a deflated lilo. (**DREW DIAL RATING 8.8/10**)

He ordered everyone out of the water with his *(very)* loudhailer. Then he put on a questionable swimming hat and dived in to rescue my dad with what looked very like a small inflatable lilo *(really?)*.

By the time the lifeguard got to the middle of the lake, my dad had resurfaced and was happily treading water. But this lifeguard wasn't giving up. He got my dad in some kind of headlock and started towing him by the neck back to the bank of the lake.

Dad was **NOT** very happy about this.

'*WHAT* EST LE PANIQUE?' shouted my dad in some strange English/French mash-up. He was really annoyed. '*Je suis une EXPERT swimmer and je suis was just about to win the loaf de lilo competition!*'

The attempt at French was getting more and more

wild with every passing second. But the lifeguard just carried on with him in the headlock until they made it back to the shore.

Which was when he attempted to give my dad mouth-to-mouth resuscitation.

'GET OFF MOI, tu es un FOOL!'

'All right, mate,' said the lifeguard when he finally let go. 'Calm down. I just saved your life.'

'Saved my life?' coughed my dad. 'You nearly choked me to death with your bare hands. Where on earth did you train to be a lifeguard? At wrestling school?'

'No. At the Oasis Leisure Centre,' he said. And before he even said it, I just knew what was coming next . . . 'In Stockport.'

Why on earth is everyone here from Stockport? I was going to ask the lifeguard about it but I didn't get a chance because everyone was staring at us, not happy that they all had to get out of the lake, and shouting, 'Perte de temps!' which is French for timewasters. We found that out when the lifeguard was only too happy to translate.

Why does this stuff only ever happen to us? And when I say *us*, I am not sure if I really mean *me*.

But it seems like it is impossible for the Drew family to have an ordinary holiday. Like one where you might just go swimming, play board games and have some barbecues. Ours has to involve berserk animals, mouth-to-mouth resuscitation and a break-off population from Stockport (*collective* **DREW DIAL RATING 10/10**).

Why? (*Head-scream.*)

Just when I thought that my dad was going to make us all get back in the car and start the journey home, a family (*I think they felt sorry for us*) asked if we wanted to borrow their gigantic inflatable flamingo.

And just like that, Lilo Loafing was **BACK ON**! The Prune **LOVED** it. Although he kept hugging the flamingo and falling in. Dad had a good attempt *(he didn't burst the inflatable this time)* and managed **42 seconds**. My mum's heart wasn't really in it. She was still too upset that we had to leave the holiday and only managed **6 seconds**. I held on for **45 seconds**. My dad wasn't happy that I had beaten him and shouted something about a refund from *'that coach'* as I sailed past **42 seconds**. *He had a lilo loafing coach?* was my only thought as I hit the lake water as the **winner**.

And then, in the BIGGEST **SURPRISE** of the holiday *(and that has some serious competition)*, Troy wanted to have a go. He said that he'd been reading a blog about balancing on a skateboard so thought that he might beat us.

Classic Troy as usual. He honestly thought that a quick browse of a skateboard website would give him the balance of a tightrope walker.

It didn't.

Troy made it to standing. But only on one leg *(which was ironic given that he was standing on a flamingo).*

The lilo slid from under him and he went **hair first** into the water.

Troy thought that this was such a **major** catastrophe. He started SCREAMING so loudly I thought we might have to declare a national emergency and call the lifeguard back.

4 p.m. – The Prune and the Sick

As we started the journey home, I spotted a sign on the road.

'Goodbye from Beziers. Twinned with Stockport, England'

Underneath it was an advert from an airline for cheap flights. It must be cheaper if you don't book the return journey and stay in Beziers. But at least this explains why half the population of Stockport live here.

And now we had **19 hours** in the car to look forward to.

Troy has just announced he's quit the skateboarding vlog.

Is it just me? But can you quit something that you have never actually started?

He said that his **audience** wanted something different from him so he needed to *'respect that'*. His *'audience'* (as far as I can see) is made up of one person. **His friend Frankie.** And knowing Frankie, I am not sure I would base the direction of my entire career on him.

I think Troy is still so **EMBARRASSED** by his lilo loafing performance he doesn't want to repeat it on a skateboard while live streaming in front of an audience. He has a point.

Either way, my mum and dad were full of praise. 'What a brave decision,' my mum said.

Followed by, 'So thoughtful and such commitment,' from my dad.

COMMITMENT?! Troy has never showed commitment to **anything** except his **hairstyle**.

This adoration for Troy clearly got too much for the Prune. He cried and then vomited half a lake's worth of water (and some green slime and possibly a small crab) all over me, Troy and the back of the car. I couldn't quite believe that so much sick could fit inside someone so small.

'Don't worry,' shrieked my mum as my dad pulled over. 'We'll be fine. We've still got three bottles of bleach in the boot.'

She leapt out of the car, a bit too excited at the

prospect of bleaching her three children if you ask me.

But of course, she couldn't find any bleach. I had swapped it for the tickets to the lake.

'Yeah,' I said, 'about that . . .'

10 August

3 p.m.

We're back.

Only 23 hours after we set off. And 10 hours after we missed the ferry. AGAIN. I mean, how many ferries can one family miss in the space of three days . . .?

Exactly how we managed to run out of petrol half a mile after passing a petrol station is a mystery that I am not sure I will ever solve. We even talked about the petrol station as we drove right past it.

I asked if we could stop to buy a snack. My mum asked how much it would cost to buy 12 snacks at 47 euro cents each. And my dad just said no, we couldn't stop.

Everyone saw the petrol station.

So 30 seconds later when the car started twerking in the middle of the road, it shouldn't have been quite as big a surprise as my dad seemed to think it was.

'Why are we slowing down? What on earth is wrong with this thing?' he shouted. 'I am going to kill Paul if he has ruined this car.'

I don't think he meant to say that last bit. And Dad started panicking when he could see the look on my mum's face.

'What has Paul been doing with the car?' she said.

At this point (and maybe to avoid Mum's line of questioning), I think he pressed the accelerator down as far as it would go.

Now . . . Is it just me? But when would adding a **MASSIVE** dose of speed to a car that was already having major problems ever be a good move?

It wasn't. Something sounded like it exploded, then the car jumped forward about two metres and came to a total stop.

EVERYTHING died – the **radio**, the **lights**, the **dashboard display**.

It was 3 a.m. We were sitting in the middle of an N road somewhere in the middle of France. In total darkness.

'*WHAT has Paul been doing with the car?*' my mum asked again. I wasn't sure that this was the right time for her to be pushing this one.

And my dad ducked the question again. He jumped out of the car and started trying to push it off the road. He was shouting for Troy to help him, but he was asleep. Quite how he had managed to sleep through the whole thing when the car was lurching along the road like an out-of-breath frog was beyond me.

Luckily *(a rare thing in the Drew family)* we were on a hill, so my dad managed to roll the car on to the verge by the side of the road on his own. And just in time as it turns out. Because seconds later, a bakery van came past us at such speed that I really think we might have been Drew sandwiches if we'd still been in the middle of the road.

All this left us with the problem of
what to do next. We talked about the
idea of **walking** back to the petrol
station to get help. But it got **so complicated**. Dad
couldn't go with Troy because he thought it might not
be safe for the rest of us back in the car. Troy couldn't
go with Mum in case that wasn't safe. It was like one of
those brain teasers where a rabbit, two foxes and a
donkey are trying to cross a river on a raft that can't
hold them all at once.

In the end, no one went to the petrol station and we
called the police. Who said they would send out a
breakdown truck.

And the wait provided the perfect opportunity for my
mum to ask her question again.

'WHAT ON EARTH has Paul got to do with this?'

My dad looked sheepish. At which point the Prune
waded in and unknowingly dropped my dad right in it.

'Daddy let Uncle Paul fix car.'

My dad looked **even more** sheepish.

'It isn't as bad as it sounds,' said Dad.

'Exactly HOW is it any better than THAT sounds?' asked Mum. 'Paul knows less about cars than he does about movies. And that is saying something! What did you let him do to the car?'

My dad really couldn't get out of answering this time, so he came clean.

'I was trying to save some money – what with the downstairs carpet and the ticket barrier minibus crash,' he explained. 'But I still wanted to get the car checked over at the garage before the holiday journey. It would have been a hundred and eight pounds though.'

'And well, Paul said he'd save me some money and do the service himself for fifty pounds,' continued Dad. 'It was a bit strange. He was SO keen to do it. He did spend ages on it though.'

'Yeah,' said Troy, who appeared to have woken up.

'But he asked to borrow my phone while he was doing it and I found a YouTube video called "How to Change the Oil in a Nissan Qashqai" when he gave it back.'

'Did EVERYBODY know about Uncle Paul the cut price mechanic EXCEPT ME?' screamed Mum.

I certainly didn't. Leave me well out of this one. I would have known it was a **TERRIBLE** idea.

At that moment, a large green tow truck arrived. The guy plugged his computer into the dashboard and a red light started flashing.

'Let me have it straight. What has he done to my car?' shouted my dad.

'I do not know who it iz you iz talking about,' replied the French mechanic in English that was definitely better than my dad's French. 'Sir, you az run out of ze petrol . . . Is you not zeeing the station de petrol just back there?'

I thought my mum was going to **explode**. With **RAGE**. At my dad for driving past a petrol station and running out of petrol half a minute later.

I thought my dad was going to **implode**. With regret. He really had not needed to tell my mum that he had employed the world's least qualified mechanic to work on our car.

5 a.m. – Burnt Hair

We MISSED the ferry. But the holiday was such a bust by then that I think everyone was past caring.

We ate six tins of beef bourguignon in the car park while we waited for the next boat. My mum even started to be a bit nicer to my dad after he said his tin was really tasty. It wasn't,

but I think he wanted to be back in her good books.

Which didn't last.

Because when we began the drive home from the

ferry, a **SERIOUS** smell of BURNING started coming from the engine.

This time there was no denying Uncle Paul's involvement.

When my dad popped the bonnet open, there it was – catching fire on top of the engine.

And it looked **suspiciously** like Uncle Paul's **WIG**.

12 August

WRAPPING FOR BRITAIN

As soon as I had slept off the holiday of all holidays, I went straight over to Priya's. There were a few things we needed to do:

1. Discuss the **Maisie Movie Masterplan**. Priya didn't know that I had **bagged us both** an invite yet.

2. Decide what we were **going to wear** to the ~~party~~ **festival** now that we were **definitely** going. It was only **ten** days away. My teeth were getting a little bit itchy again.

3. Make the **final arrangements** for our **BIG** fundraising event. **The car boot sale.** It was happening on Sunday. We **need** Edward's suggestions. He **always** has the **best ones** and after all, this fundraising event is for his stairlift, so **we need to make sure he's on board!** He's going to come over in a bit, but first I need to . . .

4. Tell her **all** about the holiday (that was **nothing** like a holiday).

Priya's dad answered the door. He was wearing GOLD **trousers** which were **way** TOO **BIG** for him and a gold medallion round his neck. He also had a baseball cap on his head that was turned round the **wrong way**. From behind him you could see that the cap was from the local garden centre. It had their logo of a compost heap on it. I'm not sure that was quite the look he was going for.

'What's going on there?' I asked.

'Don't ask,' replied Priya. 'He has been trying on outfits since yesterday. There's a new TV talent show he wants to enter called **Rap for Britain**. The audition is on Friday.'

'Right . . .' I said. 'I see.' Although I am not sure I did see.

'He's taken two whole days off work for it. One

to get dressed. One to practise his rap. My mum is going mad. Apparently he didn't take that long off work when they got married.'

Priya had some good news. While I was away, Douglas Joiner did a *sponsored hotdog-eating competition* in aid of the stairlift. His dad sponsored him £5 per hotdog. This was either very generous or shows that Douglas's dad doesn't know his son at all. Because Douglas Joiner's hero is Joey Chestnut – *world champion hotdog eater.*

Joey Chestnut can eat **75** hotdogs in **10** minutes. Which is one hotdog every 8 seconds – for 10 whole minutes (*my mum would be proud of that calculation*). It is like eating dinner for 30 people, just by yourself, and in only 600 seconds. And Douglas Joiner seems to think that this is the best skill he has ever seen. He watches videos of Joey Chestnut on YouTube all the time and even asked me if my mum could get him a discount on frankfurters from the supermarket.

Anyway, two days ago Douglas managed **12** hotdogs

in **10** minutes. I think that is quite impressive, although apparently he hasn't eaten **ANYTHING** since, which is a bit worrying. But he raised £84 in total. Which is awesome and means we are up to £4,237. I am **HOPING** the car boot sale next week might be the thing that takes us to our **target** of £5,500.

Before I had to go home for dinner, we went to ask Priya's dad if he had any last minute items that we could sell. I nearly tripped over Kate Middleton (Priya's new cat) who was clearly hiding on the stairs waiting for me. That cat has got problems with me. I can't quite work out why.

Priya's dad was in a bad mood when we found him downstairs. His gold trousers were gone and he was dressed in the grey suit he usually wears to work.

'What happened to the other outfit?' asked Priya.

'Turns out I won't be needing it after all,' he replied. Clearly very grumpy.

'Why not?' said Priya.

'Don't laugh,' he said seriously, 'but I made a mistake about the talent show. It isn't called **Rap for Britain**.'

'What is it called then?' asked Priya.

'**Wrap for Britain**, with a **W**,' he sighed. 'It's about decorating Christmas presents.'

I mean . . . This was a **DREW DIAL RATING 12/10**.

11.45 p.m. – Truffle Log

In the end, Priya asked me and Edward if we wanted to stay over. Edward couldn't because he has a wheelchair basketball match early tomorrow morning, but I couldn't say yes fast enough. Mum had been planning to use the last of the chicken chasseur tins for dinner tonight. And that's **definitely** something to be missed.

But now I have two problems (*I probably have more problems than that, but at this exact moment I have two main ones*):

1. *Priya* has fallen asleep.

2. And **Kate Middleton** won't stop jumping on my head.

Kate Middleton clearly doesn't like the fact that I am (supposed to be) sleeping in her usual space on Priya's floor. If she gets her aim right, I think she might actually knock me out.

The other problem is that now that Priya has fallen asleep, I think the midnight feast is off. We have four chocolate cookies, a bag

of wine gums and something called a truffle log under her bed ready for 00.00 a.m. Whenever we have a sleepover, the feast is a tradition. But she fell asleep at 11.37 p.m. and eating all this on my own doesn't feel quite right. I could share it with Kate Middleton but since she might be trying to kill me right now, I'm not sure that I am feeling that generous.

Kate Middleton has just landed her best jump yet. Her two front paws went in each of my eyeballs. I couldn't see for a **whole** minute. I thought I had actually gone blind. But luckily it was just dark. She managed to press the off button on the torch with one of her back paws.

I am going to have to do something about Kate. I'm not quite sure what though. You see, she will not leave Priya's bedroom. She can't. Because Prince William and Prince Charles, who are the Singh family's other cats, gang up on Kate Middleton every time she tries to go out. It hasn't been easy for her since she arrived two weeks ago. Priya's mum is a **MASSIVE** fan of the Royal Family and she had wanted to add a Prince Harry to her little regal line-up of cat princes for a while. But a trip to the vet last week had revealed a mix-up and it turns out that Prince Harry is in fact a *girl*. So there has been a *swift* name change, but Kate Middleton is so scared of William and Charles that she hasn't left Priya's room in over a week.

11.55 p.m.

I have been downstairs to get some

kitty biscuits. I thought

that might help. But

I think Kate Middleton

lured me into a trap.

Because she's now out for the

count, snoring in the middle of my blow-up mattress.

She wins.

THIS TIME.

14 August

THE TIRED DRIVEWAY

10 a.m.

A word of advice. **DON'T** eat anything called a truffle log at 1 a.m. I am not sure what was in that thing but I could still taste it **nine** hours later. And it had some chunky bits, which is making me worried that it was a treat for Kate Middleton. **Ewwwwww** . . .

My mum picked me up from Priya's to go to Uncle Paul's. Apparently he has a violin that he thinks will sell for '**big money**' *(his words)* at the car boot sale.

According to Uncle Paul, this violin belonged to Jennifer Lawrence's dad. And was given to Uncle Paul by Jennifer Lawrence herself. I doubt this is true because this is the first I've heard about Uncle Paul knowing Jennifer Lawrence. And when he handed it over, it looked very much like he'd just got it down from his loft and forgotten to clean it. *(There was a lot of*

dust and a **suspicious** name tag which said 'Paul –
Year 8' on the inside of the case. Eye-roll.) But, with the
possible celebrity connection meaning that it might sell
for a good price, I am willing to overlook this and
believe Uncle Paul's version of the origins of the violin.

I had wanted to talk to Uncle Paul about the plan for
Maisie's party. I am so pleased that he said he would do
it. But if I am being honest, the whole visit to Uncle
Paul's was a bit strange and there wasn't really a good
moment.

When we got there I could see that his Ferrari was
parked in a driveway five doors down. When I asked him
about it, he was really shifty.

'Uncle Paul, why is your car parked on someone
else's driveway?' I asked.

'Errrrrrrrrrrrrrrrrrrrrrrrrrrrm . . .' He seemed to be
pretending to choke. 'Yeah, yeah, about that,' he said as
he carried on choking, clearly trying to buy more time.
'Errr . . . it's because . . . errr . . . it needed a rest.'

'What needed a rest? The car? Or the driveway?'

'The driveway,' he said. And having composed himself, he said it again, more firmly this time. 'The driveway.'

'But a rest from what?' I said, now even more confused. 'It's concrete.'

'Yes. But these kinds of cars are heavy. Very heavy. Yes. It has an extra heavy chassis. And Dustbin Dominic from down the road said his driveway is really strong because it was reinforced with steel when they built their basement extension last year.'

This was all sounding very bizarre, and suspiciously like Uncle Paul had sold his Ferrari. But then I made the mistake of asking why Dustbin Dominic was called Dustbin Dominic. And so Uncle Paul grabbed the opportunity to change the subject as quickly as the Prune would grab a spare bag of Haribo.

'He had an argument with his wife. She was so annoyed with him that, while he was asleep, she put all his clothes in the dustbin. He went to work the next day in a suit he managed to pull out from the rubbish. He walked down the road with a half-eaten Yorkshire pudding stuck to the back of his leg.'

So that was the end of the conversation about the Ferrari and Uncle Paul's tired driveway. But it got even weirder when we went inside. Because it was only then that I noticed he was **STILL** wearing his pyjamas *(it was 2 p.m.)* and that his hair was very limp. Almost like he had lost half of it.

But, to top things off, he had no furniture in his living room. Uncle Paul used to have quite a fancy leather sofa, which my dad had always admired. Until his legs got stuck to it in last year's heatwave and my mum had to prise him off with a spatula from the kitchen.

Uncle Paul's explanation for the missing furniture,

flat-screen TV and lampshade . . . was that his new movie had needed to borrow them for the set.

What? Really? How low-budget is this movie? That they'd need to borrow Uncle Paul's sofa? It still had an imprint of my dad's thighs on the left-hand cushion.

18 August

THE DAY BEFORE THE CAR BOOT SALE

Midnight

I LOVE a car boot sale.

As of today, we've got £4,237.23. The 23 pence was raised this morning by Troy. He **promised** to do a sponsored run, but put so **LITTLE** effort in that he only got **one** sponsor *(£1 from his friend Frankie)*. He got **tired** after just **230** metres of the promised 1,000 metres. So Frankie only paid up 23 pence. It is better than nothing, I suppose.

So tomorrow's boot sale is the latest in a long line of cake sales and sponsored bike rides. But I have high hopes that this might be our biggest money maker yet *(this really is my 'thing', right?)* Because we aren't going to any old boot sale. No, **WE ARE GOING TO THE BIG ONE. THE MASSIVE ONE**. The one that's held just once a month at the cattle market on the other side of town. It is so popular that you even have to pay to get in. This is where **SERIOUS** deals are done and *(I hope)* big money changes hands.

You have to get there at **4 a.m.** to queue up for the best slots. Some people **even** arrive the **night before**. Park up with a flask of tea and a sausage roll and then sleep in their car until the gates open. My dad has flatly refused to do that. So instead of leaving in about three hours from now, we are getting there for **8 a.m.** tomorrow. I know that this is a **mistake**, but as Dad is providing the only means of transport *(thankfully not the minibus this time)*, I don't have much choice.

The whole thing has started badly though because Troy has announced he wants to come too. This is annoying for three reasons:

1. *Troy* is **annoying.**

2. *Troy* and his hair take up a lot of space in the car, meaning we won't be able to fit in the violin donated by Uncle Paul.

3. See reason 1 again.

We have had a family stand-off. I told Troy that he can't come but *(as usual)* Dad is on Troy's side. I wanted to scream when he said, *'Harper, we really could use Troy's experience in selling.'*

Is it just me? But **WHAT** experience? At selling **WHAT?** Surely Dad wasn't talking about the baked-bean chickpea fiasco? Profits still stand at ZERO on that one. Although, knowing my parents, they have probably bought all the unsold jars from Troy to spare his disappointment.

If Troy comes, I know that he will cause **chaos**. So I decided I needed to take some action. I briefly thought about locking Troy in his room. But I had two worries about this. Firstly, I didn't want to see those guys from the fire brigade again if it went wrong. Secondly, last time they said we might have to pay a fine for being a 'nuisance' and I really didn't want that to happen. It would be another setback for the downstairs carpet which would make my dad really mad. And I needed him onside to drive us to the boot sale tomorrow.

So I went out and packed the car so full that there is only room left for my dad to drive. And me to squeeze into the back between my grandad's vinyl rock collection and his heavy-metal DVDs (he says we can sell them because he only streams his music now).

There is **no** room for Troy.

OR HIS HAIR.

19 August

THE ACTUAL CAR BOOT SALE

7.30 a.m.

And guess who was sitting **ON** *(actually* **ON***)* my grandad's musical antiques?

TROY.

I didn't even **do** a **head-scream**. I **did** an ⒶⒸⓉⓊⒶⓁ scream.

But there was no persuading my dad.

So we arrived at the boot sale with Troy in the front seat. Me in the back. After a quick rearrange we strapped the violin to the roof using some piece of unidentifiable exercise equipment of my mum's. We didn't get there until 8.30 a.m. Which, as I had suspected, was **TOO LATE**, and we got a position in the *'overflow'* field.

As we pulled in, I looked around and couldn't believe just how big this thing was *(there were literally thousands of cars)*. If this place is ever actually full of cows that are for sale, I can only think that we must live in the hamburger capital of Europe.

Now there is a **STRATEGY** to an arrival at a car boot sale. It might sound strange, but ⓗⓞⓦ you open your boot is **MAKE** or **BREAK**, profits-wise. Since this could be the difference between getting the school stairlift this January and having to wait another year for the next January sale, we needed to get it right.

It must **NOT** *(for example)* go the way of our first boot sale in St Egwin's Church car park. That was a disaster. Mum wasn't concentrating and sold the decorating table for £3.50 within the first 30 seconds. The problem was that the decorating table **WASN'T** for sale. We had brought it to *display* the things we had to sell. And without it, everything was just a hot mess on the floor.

Without the table we only managed another £8.75 in sales. And Dad wasn't happy when he had to buy a new one *(for £26.99)* to decorate the Prune's bedroom two weeks later. Funnily enough, my mum didn't ask me to work out the profits on that one . . . she was unusually quiet on the maths front.

Now St Egwin's had not attracted a big crowd. But today the cattle market was packed. Which meant one thing: **DEALERS**. These are **professionals**. People who earn their **actual** living buying and selling antiques and collectible items. And the cattle market is their hunting ground, where they prey on fresh-faced families about to sell off their greatest heirlooms for less than the price of a McDonald's Happy Meal. Edward's mum has been fleeced like this before. A dealer offered her £9.50 for a rusty old set of knives and forks she'd had in the garage for years. She couldn't quite believe her luck. That was until she saw them freshly polished in the antique shop in town. On sale for £875. Apparently they had been used to feed Queen Victoria (*or something like that*). **Who knew?** Not Edward's mum as it turned out.

So I had spent the journey trying to explain to Dad

and Troy the arrival routine. Edward and Priya *(who were both meeting us there)* had rehearsed this. And it was very simple:

DO NOT OPEN THE BOOT.
I repeat: DO NOT OPEN THE BOOT.

Which sounds like a slightly strange plan. At a boot sale. But unless you get your *(new)* decorating table set up first to display the goods, the **DEALERS** will swarm in on you like locusts. And if that happened, in the chaos and panic I knew that someone would flog the Jennifer Lawrence violin way too cheap.

And, guess what?

Yep . . . it all went *(TOTALLY)* wrong.

8.45 a.m.

Troy jumped out of the car as soon as it stopped. A nearby dealer asked him to open the boot, which he did *(head-scream)* and then ran off. It turns out that he had only come with us because Jasmine Baqri's mum had a stall selling vegan shoes, which meant there was an outside chance Jasmine Baqri had been roped in to help. Jasmine Baqri is Troy's *(not so)* **secret crush**. Everything about Jasmine Baqri is beautiful, even her name. Which explains why Troy had been up blow drying his hair extra early at 6.25 a.m. today.

With the boot wide open before my dad had even put the car's handbrake on, we were finished. By the time I got out of the car, we were **swamped** with dealers. One had **even** used the wheel of Edward's wheelchair as a step to actually **climb** into the boot. That made me so **mad**.

Who sold what and for how much in that 10 minutes of complete pandemonium we'll never know. But by the end we only had half of our stock left. And it was the bad half.

AND the violin was gone.

I cried. And I might even cry again now just thinking about it. I was crushed. We had worked so hard, planned so carefully. And more than anything, I wanted to do this for Edward. Look how people treat him. Like that

dealer, basically standing on him to
get a first look at a **china hedgehog**.

    This isn't OK. **NOT OK. AT ALL.**

    I **want** the stairlift. He **needs** the
stairlift. Other people at school would really **benefit**
from the stairlift too. And now we might not be able to
afford it by January.

10 a.m.

Dad could see how upset I was. So to try to make things
better, he gave me money to get an ice cream with
Edward and Priya. We headed to the van only to realise
that my dad hadn't been feeling quite generous enough.
The ice creams were £2 each. Unless we could get three
for the price of two, someone was going to miss out.

    Edward tried first.

    'Excuse me, sir.' Edward was always **SO** polite.
*'The thing is we've got enough money for
two ice creams. But we are one pound
and twenty-five pence short for three.'*

'And?' said the guy in the van. He was quite sarcastic. This was going to be more difficult than we had thought.

'Well . . .' said Edward, trying to think of a reason why the guy in the van should help us out on this one. 'There are three of us.'

'Which is your problem, not mine,' said the van guy. He was getting annoyed now. 'What does it say on the van?'

'Erm . . .' Edward was clearly confused. 'S-Sundays are f-for Sundaes,' he stuttered.

'Are you trying to be funny?' Which Edward definitely wasn't. And it did say that in massive letters on the side of the van. 'What does it say at the TOP of the van?'

'Norman's Ice Creams limited?'

169

'Exactly. It DOES NOT say "The National Society for Giving out Free Ice Cream". I'm a business, mate. Either buy two or come back when you've got enough money for three.' The van guy was almost shouting now.

This was going seriously sideways. And a massive queue was forming behind us.

Priya suggested she go back to the car and get the 'antique' ice-cream scoop that her dad had donated to us. She thought the van guy might be tempted to trade a third ice cream for this lovely item. But this was a bad idea because:

1. I had **serious doubts** that the scoop was antique. The dealers hadn't wanted it. And it said '**IKEA**' on the handle.

2. **Norman the van man** sold Mr Whippy. There wasn't any expensive, home-made ice cream in sight. **He wasn't a man that needed a scoop.**

3. By the time Priya got to the car and back, the

van guy could have called the **police** and had us **arrested for timewasting.**

But then I had a 𝔹ℝ𝕀𝕃𝕃𝕀𝔸ℕ𝕋 idea. I was so excited that I even forgot I was upset about the Jennifer Lawrence violin for a minute.

'We'll take four cones,' I said.

'Hang on. I thought you couldn't even pay for two?' snapped Norman the van guy.

'We can,' I said, although I was a bit worried about this. What I had in mind was quite risky.

'Well, then pay me first.'

'Here's the money for two,' I said, handing over £4. 'Make those and I'll have the money for the third by the time you've finished.'

Norman rolled his eyes and made the first cone. As soon as he handed it to me I sprinted to the back of the now ginormous queue.

'Fresh ice cream. No need to queue. Only three pounds twenty-five!' I shouted.

It was way easier than I thought. One guy said he'd left his stall unattended, handed me £4.50 straight away then sprinted off. I think I could have held out for £5.

Back at the van, Norman seemed to be quite impressed when I handed over the money for two more ice creams.

'Do you want a job?' he asked.

I think he was serious.

1 p.m.

Troy appeared from the vegan shoe stall a few hours later. *(I do wonder about a vegan shoe stall at a cattle market. Is it weird? Or would the cows quite like the idea? I can't decide what I think about that.)*

Anyway, I was so angry I could hardly look at Troy when he arrived back at the car. But when I did, I saw that he was carrying something.

It was a basketball hoop.

And not even a good basketball hoop. It was bent.

'Wow, Troy! That looks amazing.

I LOVE basketball. How much was it?' Dad asked him with a look of glowing admiration that brought tears to my eyes.

'Nothing,' Troy said proudly. *'I swapped that old violin for it.'*

20 August

THE PESTIVAL

I am still angry. We only made £75.50 at the boot sale, which is much less than I had hoped. We are still £1,187.27 short for the stairlift. That is A LOT of **sponsored jogs, head-shaves, cake-bakes** and **race-your-favourite-slug** events to organise before Christmas.

I may **NEVER** speak to Troy again.

Edward thinks I can hold a grudge for too long though. He might be right. I *am* still upset with Toby Flood for killing my pet goldfish, Kanye West. He'd been happily swimming around his bowl when Toby Flood decided he wanted a cuddle. Let's just say Kanye West didn't survive very long in Toby's fat fingers. But we were only three at the time and Toby Flood hadn't really understood the importance of water . . . to Kanye West. So maybe Edward is right and it is time to let that one go?

Maisie has started to be a bit of a **pest** about the arrangements for filming her party/festival . . . or

. . . **PESTIVAL** as I have started calling it. She keeps texting instructions for Uncle Paul to my mum's phone. It is starting to annoy Mum. I am hoping that this might be what tips her into letting me have a phone of my own.

The latest text to come through said:

> Harper, tell your uncle Phil and his team that he will need to make time for at least five outfit changes. PS Might wear that camouflage outfit you gave me at your birthday. M xxx

I DID NOT give her that outfit. I'm not sure where she got that idea. I lent it to her to save the situation after Priya was sick all over Maisie at my birthday. It explains why she hasn't given it back though.

These arrangements will need some COREFUL management with Uncle Paul. I have told him it will only take an hour of his Saturday. Maisie clearly has other ideas.

And it might also need some careful management of Maisie too. I don't think Uncle Paul is bringing a **'team'** with him. Unless Leonardo DiCaprio makes an appearance *(the dog, not the actor).*

I am not going to be able to match five outfit changes either. I am not sure I have **two** party outfits, let alone **five**. And if she is keeping the combat outfit, I might be down to one.

22 August

KRUNCHY KREAMS

9 a.m.

I think my mum is feeling sorry for me after all the texts from Maisie.

Another one arrived this morning.

> Harper, can you arrive at 1 p.m. to help set everything up? PS Bring some Krunchy Kream doughnuts. M xx

Krunchy Kreams are sold at a **really** expensive bakery in town. I have only ever seen one when Uncle Paul brought some round for the Prune's birthday last year. Each doughnut had a **whole** Mars bar on the top. My mum has already said we are **NOT** buying any.

BUT she has offered to take me shopping to buy a present for Maisie **AND** a new outfit. Which is **AWESOME**.

Buying something for Maisie is a **NIGHTMARE** though.

She has everything already. At least everything I could ever imagine anyway. And the Drew family savings are already allocated – to the downstairs carpet, the back windscreen wiper and the repair bill from the ticket barrier crash. So I know I am not going to have a big budget for this present.

Last year Edward thought he had nailed it. He spent quite a lot of his pocket money on a **bonsai tree**. Who has one of those? And who wouldn't want one? At least that's what Edward thought, until he saw it for sale in the charity shop near Maisie's house the day after her party.

It still had the tag on it:

Happy birthday, Maisie.
From Edward x

10.30 a.m. – Uncle Paul and the Car Park

The shopping trip was a major success. I think.

I got two outfits. My mum was feeling generous after she asked me if I could calculate the volume of the changing room. I said the words *'three cubic metres'* and that was enough . . . she was at the counter buying both the outfits I wanted.

We bought Maisie a set of **bath bombs.** They are in the shape of doughnuts. So I am hoping that might make up for the fact that Mum isn't buying the Krunchy Kreams.

On the way home, the usual happened.

We were already on the roundabout and had gone past the exit for the supermarket. But then my mum seemed to remember herself and did an extra loop back to the turning while saying something about needing some feta cheese and a sink plunger.

But it wasn't until we were on the way out that I saw something odd. **REALLY ODD.**

We had been in the supermarket for ages. My mum spent so long swapping tins of kidney beans around on their shelf for something she called the 'optimal sales display'. I have no idea what she meant. But I am fairly sure that no one even likes kidney beans anyway.

We were at the till paying when the manager of the supermarket came racing over.

'Excuse me, madam. We have just been watching you on our CCTV,' he said to my mum.

MY HEART SANK. This probably meant that we weren't getting out of here **any time soon**. And I really wanted to get home and show Priya my new outfits.

'Why?' said my mum with a kilo of feta cheese in one hand and a sink plunger in the other. She did look weird, so I wasn't surprised that they had picked her out on the security camera.

'Because no one has ever shown that much interest in kidney beans before . . . so we . . . ermmmm . . . wondered whether there might be some suspicious activity going on . . .'

My mum lost it.

She thrust the plunger forward as she started to

shout at the manager. The rubber end
was **SO CLOSE** to his face that I worried if she went
any further she might connect with his mouth and
accidentally **SUCK OUT** what he'd had for lunch.

Once the manager realised that she worked in
non-fresh produce at head office *(and that his shelves
were in a mess)*, his whole **attitude** was different. He
dropped the *'we might arrest you'* tone and went with
a **major charm** offensive instead.

He gave her a £20 voucher for *'being a good
customer'*, which meant that we would almost certainly
be back here tomorrow to spend it *(my mum was so
happy)*.

He even insisted on carrying the feta and the plunger out to our car for us.

Which was when I thought I saw Uncle Paul.

But surely it couldn't be him? Could it?

He was getting out of a bashed-up old car, parked opposite ours. And he looked as if he was wearing the supermarket uniform.

My mum was engrossed in her conversation with the manager about the benefits of displaying Marmite crisps next to actual Marmite *(for something called 'cross sell')* that she didn't notice.

I decided to go over and see if it really was him.

But when he saw me he dived back in the car and put his coat on. *'Harper?'* he said, zipping up his coat. *'What are you doing here?'*

'On the daily trip to the supermarket with Mum,' I sighed.

'Of course you are. What essential items could she not live without today?' he asked, shoving what looked like a name badge into his pocket.

'Feta cheese and a sink plunger.'

'Well, you never know when you'll need to eat a Greek salad while fixing a blocked toilet,' he said with a smile. *'Anyway, I had better go.'*

'What are you doing here, Uncle Paul?' I asked.

'Errrmmmmm . . .' He paused. *'Buying supplies for the film crew,'* he added quickly. *'We're filming a scene in a corner shop today so I . . . errrrr . . . need to get the stuff to fill the set.'*

REALLY? Would a Hollywood producer have to go and buy the chocolate bars and loo rolls himself? Don't they have whole teams for that sort of thing?

'Come over and say hi to Mum – she might even give you her £20 voucher,' I said. We both knew she definitely wouldn't do that. That would mean she had no excuse to come back tomorrow.

'I can't, Harper. It's one minute to two. And I have to be in the store by two.' And Uncle Paul raced off into the shop, through a side door that said 'Staff Only'.

Before I walked back to my mum chatting to the manager, I had a look through the window of Uncle Paul's car. It was an even **BIGGER MESS** than Troy's bedroom. There were sandwich wrappers all over the passenger seat and there was a duvet and a pillow in the back.

And a pair of **pyjamas**.
And a Superman **toothbrush**.
And a picture of Leonardo DiCaprio. In a **heart-shaped frame**.

3.15 p.m. – Car Napping

After we got back from the **bizarre** shopping trip, I went over to show Priya my pestival outfits. Luckily Edward was there because I wanted to talk to both of them about Uncle Paul. After what I saw this morning at the supermarket, I am a bit worried about him.

I tried to talk to Mum about it in the car on the way home, but she was so excited about the conversation with the store manager that she wasn't really listening. Roger *(the manager)* had invited my mum back to the store **'ANY TIME'** to talk about his shelves. She was so happy about this that I think Mum might have a small crush on him. He does have her dream job after all.

I wonder whether Roger will be quite as happy as she is when he realises that **'ANY TIME'** is quite likely to mean **'ALL THE TIME'** with my mum.

Uncle Paul must be sleeping in his car and working at the supermarket. So what has happened to his house? And the movies he is supposed to be making? And where is Leonardo DiCaprio *(the dog, not the actor)*?

Priya agreed with me. *'Why else would there be a toothbrush and a duvet on the back seat?'*

Edward thinks that there might be another explanation. Edward is always looking on the bright side. He thinks that maybe it is tiring working on a movie set, so it could be good to have a nap in the car when it gets late on set. *'That's why they have trailers,'* Edward said.

Maybe? But trailers are usually quite big and nice. Uncle Paul is sleeping in a bashed-up old car where he can't possibly fully stretch his legs out. So I have my doubts. And anyway, that still doesn't explain why he was dressed like he was about to start work on the supermarket checkout?

And why doesn't he just come clean and tell us if this is his new job?

Something isn't right with Uncle Paul. I just know it.

24 August

BATH BOMB

Troy. TROY. TROY ...

Has risen to **new** levels of **annoying**.

Last night he invited Frankie round to help him with his new vlog. He and Frankie spent all night testing new ideas that might work for his *'audience'*. His **audience** of one person — **Frankie**.

The new idea might actually be something that could work though. Because as far as I can tell, it seems to be about finding ways to do things with the **LEAST** amount of effort. And Troy is **already** a world expert at that.

He wants to call it Troyz Life Hackz. And if you ask me, he hasn't put much effort into thinking of that title. So he's starting as he means to go on.

The first thing Troy and Frankie wanted to try was some cooking — without the effort of using a cooker. So they decided to see if they could fry an egg on the bonnet of our car. It was a pretty hot day, but it definitely wasn't hot enough. Somehow they even convinced Dad to turn the car engine on to see if that would help. It didn't. But they still filmed 12 eggs sliding slowly down the bonnet and dribbling on to the driveway.

Obviously, they didn't bother to clean any of it up. And now, in the heat, the smell of old egg is beginning to get really disgusting.

And is it just me . . . but even if you *could* fry an egg on the bonnet of a car, why would that be a good thing? Who wants to eat an egg that may or may not have been cooked in bird poop, engine oil or windscreen wash?

Now they have filled the paddling pool up and are trying to see if they can stay dry if they wrap themselves in cling film. An episode they are planning to call *'Who Needs a Towel?'*.

I can hear Troy saying to the camera, *'If this works in the paddling pool, it will work in the shower. Just think about how much time you'll save when you come out already dry, guys.'*

I mean . . . **Seriously?**

There is **so much wrong** with this that I don't know where to start:

1. **Drying** yourself with a **towel** doesn't even take that long.

2. It **definitely** takes less time than **wrapping** your whole body in **cling film** every time you take a bath.

3. And . . . I am not sure **how** you are supposed to **wash** when you're covered in **plastic**.

4. Troy needs a **towel** for his **hair** routine anyway.

But there they are. SITTING in the paddling pool. WRAPPED in cling film.

What I can't work out is why the water in the paddling pool is a **dark** shade of **brown**. Troy showers **SO** often to wash his hair that it couldn't be anything to do with him. Frankie is a bit more of a concern on the cleanliness front, but I still can't imagine that he could turn that much water brown.

I shout out of the window to ask. The reply is definitely not what I wanted to hear.

'Frankie found five bath bombs in the kitchen.

He thought they were doughnuts but he started foaming at the mouth when he took a bite.'

Troy and Frankie think this is hilarious.

'We chucked them all in here to see what colour the water would go.'

NIGHTMARE . . . Now I have ∩© present for Maisie!

25 August
BOXED UP

I was still really **worried** about Uncle Paul after the incident at the supermarket a few days ago. So when my mum said she was going to the post office to return a shower cap she'd bought online, I said that I would go with her.

I knew that she wouldn't just be going to the post office. There would definitely be a trip to the supermarket involved. And that might give me a chance to see Uncle Paul and check he was OK. Last time, he had seemed so desperate to make me think that everything was fine. When it clearly wasn't.

Sure enough, as soon as the shower cap had been dispatched back to Dryzabone *(which sounded like a business Troy would be involved with)*, we were on our way to the supermarket to see whether they had any **'bigger'** shower caps in stock. I didn't ask about the shower cap sizing problems my mum seemed to be having *(does she have a massive head?)* I just couldn't get into that right now. Because I had already spotted Uncle Paul's car in the car park. So he was definitely here somewhere.

As soon as we got inside the shop, Mum made a run for the pasta aisle. She said she needed to check whether they were stocking the four different types of rigatoni required by head office. Which gave me the perfect opportunity to go looking for Uncle Paul.

It didn't take me long. I checked the bakery first *(he loves a cake so that would be his ideal job)* but then I **saw him** on the till.

And Uncle Paul spotted me too. He **DIVED** underneath the conveyor belt in an **attempt** to **hide**. But the man he was serving started to get agitated that his four steaks and four grapefruits *(that's going to be one weird meal)* were not being scanned. The customer was threatening to call a manager, so Uncle Paul had no choice but to get up from under the till. When he did . . . he had a cardboard box *(one of the boxes you carry* *bottles in)* . . . on his head.

'Sorry, sir,' I could hear him explaining. 'I just bent down to pick up my pen and accidentally got this stuck on my head. Hazard of the job.'

This was getting out of control.

'Uncle Paul, I know it's you,' I said. 'Why are you hiding from me?'

Reluctantly he took the box off his head. He looked **terrible**. Like he hadn't slept for a week.

'Hi, Harper, great to see you. Can't really talk now though,' he said. 'Just covering a shift for a friend who usually works here but had to have emergency surgery on his middle toenail.'

Too much information.

'Are you OK, Uncle Paul?' I kept trying. 'It's just that you seem a bit . . .' I was slightly lost for words at this point . . . all over the place . . .

'Harper, honestly, I am fine. No need to worry about me at all. I love it here. They give me the leftover bakes at the end of the day. Yesterday I had

two cream horns and a freshly made scotch egg . . .
Anyway, are we all set for tomorrow? For the movie?
I am so excited that you asked me to do it. I am
really looking forward to getting out and doing some
filming again . . .' He trailed off.

I don't think that he meant to let it slip that he
hadn't been doing much filming lately. It was kind of
obvious though and I felt so sorry for him. But I could
tell that he really didn't want me to, so I decided to
ditch the questioning. I was just thrilled that he seemed
genuinely pleased about the **Maisie Movie Masterplan**.

'Do me one favour, Harper? Don't tell Eve – I mean
your mum – that you saw me,' he said. 'She'll have a
million questions and then she'll want to compare
staff discounts. I just don't think I've got the energy
for that.'

'It's not going to be easy keeping this under wraps,
Uncle P – she is in here literally every day. She is a
hazard of the job, right there.'

Talking of which, I could see my mum coming down

the shampoo aisle carrying two huge shower caps while deep in conversation with Roger *(the supermarket manager)*, who seemed to be making some kind of hand gesture about the size of my mum's head. She was so engrossed in the chat that there was no way she would have noticed Uncle Paul anyway.

But . . . it seemed like he wasn't willing to take the risk.

Because when I looked round to say goodbye . . . the box was **back** on his head.

26 August

GOING TO THE PESTIVAL

10.15 a.m.

Today is the day.

And there have been two more texts since last night.

> Have you got the Krunchy Kreams? M xx

No. And I don't even have a present for you now that Troy and Frankie wasted the bath bombs in their cling-film paddling-pool experiment. They haven't even bothered to empty the paddling pool, so it is still there as one big murky reminder of what Maisie's present used to be.

> My dad wants to know if your Uncle Paul needs parking for his trailer? Mx

Unlikely, I think. I am fairly sure there is no trailer, but there is a very messy bashed-up blue car.

My mum has now turned her phone off. She's really had enough of Maisie this time. So there is no chance of asking her if we can buy a new birthday present.

I went round to Priya's to see if she had any good ideas. She didn't. Mainly because she was a bit distracted by her dad rapping in the spare bedroom. He was practising for his class, which he starts just after he drops me and Priya at Maisie's. And the gold trousers were back on. The rap lessons are definitely no longer a secret.

'Yo, bro, I dunno, Where to go,
I'm so, Full of woe, Y'know!'

He was shouting this from upstairs.

Apparently he wrote this rap himself. It didn't sound too bad to me. Although, as my dad would say, he probably shouldn't give up his day job just yet.

Priya's mum was trying to drown out the sound of the rapping by having the radio on very loudly while cleaning her set of Royal Family teapots. She was scrubbing Prince Edward's face very hard to the beat of 'Wannabe' by the Spice Girls.

She asked me why I was looking a bit fed up. When I told her about the bath bombs she rushed off saying she had the perfect solution and came back with something from her royal china collection.

It was a mug. On the front, it had the words 'Sparkle like Princess Markle' in pink neon glittery writing with a very glossy picture of Meghan on her wedding day.

'I got given three when it was the royal wedding,' said Priya's mum. 'You can give Maisie one of these!'

It was really kind of her. And it was my only option.

Will Maisie like it?

Probably not.

But after all her texts, maybe *(just maybe – teeth itching)* I don't care that much any more.

I am not sure I mean that last bit.

1 p.m.

When Maisie opened the door, she was wearing the exact same navy blue jumpsuit as me.

NIGHTMARE.

Secretly though, I was quite **pleased**. I always thought Maisie wore way **better** clothes than me. But this proved that we **did** shop in the same places after all. And that made me *(annoyingly)* happy.

'Nice outfit, Princess,' was the first thing that Maisie said. She didn't even say hello.

I must have looked a bit too pleased with this comment, because she followed up quickly with, *'But I won't be wearing this for the actual festival. Obvs. This is my setting-up outfit. In case I get messy. It doesn't matter if I get this dirty.'*

Don't cry. **DO NOT** cry.

Priya squeezed my arm. She was trying to be nice to me, but she went with quite a firm grip to my funny bone which actually made one or two tears spill out of my eyes.

Maisie didn't notice anyway.

'Did you bring the Krunchy Kreams?' she asked, moving swiftly on.

'Not exactly . . .' I was trying to think of a good reason why I hadn't brought them. I couldn't tell her that we were saving for a new downstairs carpet and so my mum had refused to buy them.

I was wishing that I had made better use of the 48 hours since she had sent the text asking for them. To think of a proper, believable excuse. Instead I went with, 'They only had the liquorice ones left. And . . . well . . . I thought that no one likes liquorice and who wants to risk black teeth at a party?'

Which wasn't bad, I thought.

But Maisie looked pretty annoyed.

'It's a **FESTIVAL**,' she said.

I tried to save the situation by handing over the birthday gift. I am not sure why I thought that would make things any better. And it didn't.

Maisie opened it, took one look at the mug, handed it off to the AA (of course they were already there) and said, 'Sweet. Thanks, Harper. My grandma will love that for Christmas.'

Me and Priya followed Maisie into the kitchen. Douglas
Joiner was already in there. He was mopping the floor. I
had a bad feeling about this.

And I was right. Maisie handed us a bucket
and a squeegee.

'My mum asked me to clean the floors and the
windows before the festival, but I haven't had time.
And now I need to go and do my hair.' She had a
really sickly smile on her face. 'You guys don't mind, do
you? I'll let you share a tent with me.'

So . . . we ended up outside the house . . . cleaning
the downstairs toilet window.

'Why are we doing this?' I asked Priya. We were
covered in soapy water after she accidentally stood on
the bucket and tipped it over our shoes.

'Because we are fools,' said a voice from behind us.
It was Douglas Joiner, who was now weeding the front
lawn.

It turns out he was right (for once).

2 p.m. – Pestival Panic

When everything was set up, it looked **AMAZING**.

I have never seen anything like it in my life. I am sure that even if I live until I am 150, I will never have a party quite as good as this one.

Maisie's garden is the size of a football pitch. And it was full of little tepees for everyone to sleep in. There were fairy lights hanging everywhere and a van serving burgers and hotdogs. There was a magician doing tricks and a band were setting up on the patio.

It was **AWESOME**.

2.15 p.m.

Although now, not everything was going smoothly. Douglas Joiner had gone **too big, too early** on the chocolate fountain and was throwing up in the downstairs toilet. And Daniel Muldoon was heading to A & E. He had been trying to impress Maisie and the AA with a somersault on the bouncy castle but misjudged his flip and knocked out two of his teeth with his own knees.

I looked inside Maisie's tepee, which had a huge M on the side of it. There were five beds in there. But the names on the pillows *(specially sewn in)* definitely did NOT say *Harper* or

Priya. So it looked like we might not be sharing with

with Maisie after all. So the window cleaning had been for nothing. Priya would be furious.

4 p.m.

Everyone was here.

Except Uncle Paul.

He was now **TWO HOURS LATE**. Maisie was already on to her second outfit change and I wouldn't be able to make excuses for very much longer. I'd told her Uncle Paul must have been having issues on set with Jennifer Lawrence's stunt double. But time was really ticking if he was going to be able to film the best parts of the party and then make it into a film ready for the premiere tomorrow.

Edward said he would keep watch out front and make sure he got Uncle Paul in as soon as he arrived.

5.15 p.m.

Edward texted Priya to tell me he needed me urgently. He wasn't wrong.

Uncle Paul had arrived. As I had suspected, there was no trailer. Or camera crew. And he did not look as if he had come off a Hollywood film set either. In fact, he

looked (*and smelled*) very much as if he had come straight off an eight-hour shift on the fish counter at the supermarket.

He needed somewhere to change. **ASAP**. So Edward, Priya and I sneaked him in the front door and into the downstairs toilet. We thought that this would be a good place for Uncle Paul to freshen up, but the smell of fish guts and Douglas Joiner's vomit was all too much for Priya and she fainted.

Edward was all over it though.

He managed to break her fall so she didn't hit crack her head on the sink and he had a cold compress on her forehead before Uncle Paul had even removed his 'Can I Help You?' badge. He is basically **already** a **doctor**.

With Priya laid out on the floor, Uncle Paul had to go change in the back seat of his car. Which was also not all that fresh. It was still full of empty sandwich wrappers and half-eaten chocolate bars. I thought I saw the end of a Cornish pasty stuck to the duvet, but I wasn't sure I really wanted to investigate that too closely. There wasn't time.

Uncle Paul emerged looking more respectable than I had dared to hope. He put some big black sunglasses on *(very Hollywood)*, and then got a massive light and a tripod out of the boot. He even had one of those boards that you snap closed when you say *'action'*.

Maisie's Movie

He'd already written *'Maisie's Movie'* on it.

Maybe this was going to be OK after all?

5.30 p.m.

When we got back to the party, everything was going pretty well. Douglas Joiner had recovered and was on the bouncy castle. A **RISKY** choice, but he seemed **OK**. And Priya had come round and was helping Maisie's mum to put the candles on the cake.

Obviously, as soon as Uncle Paul walked in, Maisie asked where the camera crew was. She looked less than impressed when Uncle Paul told her he was going to make the film using his iPad. But he showed her some very fancy app which did look like some serious movie-making software, and then he set up his light and his tripod. He actually looked like he might have done this before.

7.15 p.m.

For about two hours things went to plan. Maisie had **five** outfit changes, **three** different hairstyles and pouted about **two** million times into the camera. Uncle Paul did some arty filming of the tepees as the sun was

starting to go down and then interviewed everyone at the party, asking them to name **three** things they liked best about Maisie.

'AMAZING', '**LIT**', 'GENEROUS', 'AWESOME', '**SLAYS**', 'SMART' and '**ON FIRE**' were said by almost everyone in different combinations.

I wasn't quite sure what to say when I was asked.

Maisie had been **SO** annoying in the run-up to the pestival. And she had **made** me and Priya clean the windows.

But now that the party was happening, it *was* pretty amazing.

Douglas Joiner said, *'The chocolate fountain, the hotdog van . . .'* But didn't manage to get to a third before he ran off to be sick **again**. His career as a competitive eater was looking seriously doubtful.

The band were getting ready to play **'HAPPY BIRTHDAY'**. Priya was still inside helping Maisie's mum with the cake. I couldn't understand what was taking her so long. **Until I saw the cake.** IT WAS HUGE. There were so many **candles**, **fireworks** and **sparklers** on the top of it that the display was likely to be as **big** as the one from the London Eye on New Year's Eve.

And this is where it all went wrong.

The cake had its own special tepee. **Of course it did.**
With fairy lights and swirling material down each side.
And on top, at the pointy bit, was a huge gold M. If
you looked quickly you might have mistaken it for the
golden arches of a McDonald's. But I wasn't going to tell
Maisie that.

Everyone crowded under the special cake tepee in
front of Maisie to sing **'Happy Birthday'**. I was with
Edward and Priya just to the side of Maisie with Uncle
Paul, who said that this was the best angle to film from.
Maisie's mum lit the candles. But I could see what was
going to happen almost before it did.

The cake was fizzing and popping with **sparks** flying everywhere. But one firework went **rogue**. Instead of staying fixed to the cake, it **SHOT** back over Maisie's shoulder and **landed** in the swirls of material covering the tepee pole. And it started to **catch fire**. And so did Maisie's **hair**, which after three hairstyle changes and several cans of hairspray was **SERIOUSLY** flammable.

'*Oh my god!*' I shouted to Edward and Priya. '*Maisie's hair is on FIRE!*'

Because everyone else was in front of Maisie, they couldn't see the disaster happening behind her. No one had noticed that anything was wrong. I needed to do something before we had a real problem. NOW.

And I was quick.
I grabbed an ice bucket, which
had been cooling cans of
drinks by the hotdog van.

It was **really**
heavy but I
managed to
swing it
upwards and
throw the
cold water
on to the fire.
AND Maisie's head.
AND all over the cake.

AND a lot on the AA, who were *(of course)* standing close to Maisie.

It wasn't the best aim, but I did stop the fire.

So I thought I would be the hero. I had just **saved** Maisie's life.

I was kind of expecting applause and maybe the prime spot in Maisie's tepee for the night. Next to Maisie.

But I was seriously **wrong** about that. Nobody else except Edward, Priya and Uncle Paul had seen the fire, so it basically looked *(to them)* as if I had chucked a bucket of cold water over Maisie and her cake for no reason.

And this seemed to prove that I was the fool Maisie had thought I was all along.

Maisie was screaming her head off. It was so loud and her head was **shaking** so much that I thought it might **actually** come off.

She was **DRENCHED**.

Her hair was stuck to her forehead

and black eye make-up was running down her face, which was bright red from shouting. She would have looked great at a Halloween party. But now was probably not the right time to mention that.

The cake was **totally ruined** too. The water had made the burnt-out fireworks smudge a big charcoal mess over the picture of Maisie on top of the cake. It kind of looked like she had a hairy black beard round her face.

'What on earth did you do that for, HARPER?' she screeched. 'YOU HAVE RUINED EVERYTHING!'

The AA looked furious. I could tell they were going on the counter-attack (why was no one realising that I had saved Maisie's life?) as Amelie or Amelia (they were so drenched it was difficult to tell who was who) launched a whole bottle of Coke towards me.

Thankfully Priya and Edward came to my rescue. They moved in front of me to make a kind of human shield and as the bottle came spinning towards my face, Edward punched it away. It landed (then **EXPLODED**) in the chocolate fountain, where Uncle Paul had stopped filming and was now coating a strawberry for himself.

And for a few short seconds, I think it actually rained **chocolate** and **Coke**.

But only Douglas Joiner seemed impressed with this latest development. I think he might have even tried to lick Uncle Paul's suit, which was now very **brown**. And very **sticky**.

'I knew I should NEVER have invited you!' Maisie screeched again. *'GET OUT. GET OUT. GET OUT! AND TAKE YOUR UNCLE PHIL WITH YOU! HE ISN'T A MOVIE PRODUCER. HE WAS SWEEPING THE AISLES AT THE SUPERMARKET WHEN WE WERE IN THERE YESTERDAY!'*

Uncle Paul looked sad, which made me really angry with Maisie. How dare she say those things to him when he was here to do something nice for her? I wanted to get him out of here — and quickly. But I was too busy trying to explain what had happened to Maisie's mum. It was no use. She wasn't listening. **It was all over**. And we were going to have to leave as if we were losers when honestly I felt like I deserved a medal. Or at the very least a thank you.

But . . . I should have known . . . this was classic Maisie Felix. And I am done trying to be on Team Maisie.

This really is up there on the **DREW DIAL RATINGS**. A full **10/10**. And I am not even quite sure who I am rating here. **MAISIE** for being such a diva? Or **ME**? For thinking she would have been any different.

As we were leaving, I could hear someone saying, *'Are you sure I can't have a slice of that cake?'*

It was Douglas Joiner.

There might be another vomit coming on.

This situation has left a very bad taste, *so . . . **this time it could be me.***

8 p.m. – Hotdog Tears

There was no talking on the walk home.

I was in such shock I could barely breathe, let alone speak.

Uncle Paul had grabbed two hotdogs from the van as

we were being chased out of the party. He had stuffed them into his mouth so fast before we set off that Douglas Joiner (and possibly even Joey Chestnut) would have been impressed. But his mouth was so full that I didn't think he could swallow them and both his **cheeks** looked like they were going to **BURST**. It would have been funny. But nobody was in the mood to laugh.

Priya and Edward were just behind me. I was pleased when they decided to leave with us. And even more pleased when Priya turned round at the gate and shouted to the party, 'Mrs Felix, ask your daughter who really cleaned all of the windows earlier!'

Maisie gave Priya a stare that made it clear that next year's invite was definitely not happening.

As we left, James Merrison could be heard shouting, 'The Princess of Dorkness strikes again!'

But Priya and Edward both rolled their eyes and said

at the exact same time, *'He's the dork!'* Which gave me a tiny glimmer of hope that I wasn't the giant loser that Maisie *(and everyone else)* seemed to think I was.

Thank goodness for the **Triple Threat**.

8.06 p.m.

When we got back home, Dad was waiting behind the front door. Pretending to be a spy. Wearing a bow tie and a black suit. He must have seen us leaving Maisie's from the upstairs bathroom window and raced down into position. Because he couldn't have been wearing that outfit for any other reason than to impress Uncle Paul. He was supposed to be regrouting the bathroom tiles. Not a job to be doing in your best suit.

Uncle Paul pushed the door open with quite a bit of force, clearly quite grumpy. He didn't see my dad as he attempted to surprise us by leaping from behind the door shouting the words, *'The name's BOND . . . Steve Bo—'* But before he could finish, the corner of the door hit my dad right on the nose. Which exploded with blood.

All over the downstairs carpet.

And that was it. For Uncle Paul.

He collapsed in a heap. And started crying. Massive tears (*which I think smelled slightly of hotdog*). All over the downstairs carpet.

When he had finished crying, which was about an hour and one very wet carpet later, my mum managed to get Uncle Paul up off the floor and into the kitchen for a cup of tea. And he started to explain why he had been acting weird for the last few weeks (*well, weirder than usual at least*).

It was a long story. And there was a LOT of crying. And it was pretty awful. But . . . these are the basics: ⬇

1. He **borrowed** a massive chunk of money from the bank so he could start **producing movies**.

2. Feeling good about all of the money in his bank account, he **rented** a bright orange **Ferrari** he couldn't afford, **bought** a **diamond** thumb ring from a guy he met on a park bench and spent **£1,000** on a blond **wig**. So that **was** what we found when the car broke down.

3. He brought **Chris Hemsworth** over from **Australia** to start filming.

4. But he **didn't realise** that producing movies is actually quite **hard**.

5. And **expensive**.

6. So the **money ran out**.

7. So he couldn't **afford** Chris Hemsworth any more.

8. But the **movie** was only **half finished**.

9. He started **selling** everything he owned to get enough money to bring Chris back to **finish** the **filming**.

10. He **rented** the **Ferrari** to **Dustbin Dominic** down the road.

11. **Sold** all his **furniture**.

12. **Moved out** of his house the day after he gave us his one remaining item – the **violin. That. Troy. Gave. Away.**

13. Tried to sell the **thumb ring** but it turned out to be a **toe ring** so nobody wanted it.

14. **Bought** a really **cheap** car (from the same guy who sold him the ring . . . you'd have thought he might have learnt his lesson there).

15. **Parked** it at the **supermarket**.

16. **Moved** into the **back seat**.

17. And got **two** jobs at the supermarket. **One** on the till. **One** on the fish counter.

But Uncle Paul left the **WORST** bit until last. And I

don't mean the bit about him losing his wig in our car engine.

He had to give **Leonardo DiCaprio** to a dog refuge because there wasn't enough room for him on the back seat of the car. And he couldn't really afford to feed him anyway. He has been visiting him twice a day.

My mum started to cry. My dad looked pretty sad too. Although it was a bit hard to tell because he had a huge tissue stuffed up each of his nostrils to stop his nosebleed.

I just felt a bit like a fool. I had been obsessed with getting invited to Maisie's party and worrying about stupid things like Krunchy Kreams. When Uncle Paul was basically homeless. And he had left his shift on the fish counter early to come and make a TV show of Maisie's party when he could barely afford to eat. He wanted to sell his iPad as well, but had kept it just so he could help me out.

His **DREW DIAL RATING** has gone down *(a first in the Drew family)* to **9/10**.

'Move in here with us, Paul,' said my mum.

She obviously hadn't discussed this with my dad because he let out a snort of surprise so loud that one of the tissues up his nostrils shot out into his cup of tea. And then his nose started to bleed again.

'Yes, definitely move in here,' said my mum again, clearly not feeling any need to get my dad's input, 'and I can drive you to the supermarket for your shifts.'

Honestly . . . any . . . opportunity . . . for a supermarket visit . . .

'Well, I do quite enjoy that job at the supermarket,' said Uncle Paul.

'But where will we all sleep?' said Troy, who had just appeared at the door wearing full school uniform – including his tie and his school shoes. It was still the middle of the holidays.

'Why are you dressed like that?' asked my dad in a bit of a panic. I think he thought he might have got his dates wrong again and we had missed the start of the school term.

Troy looked confused by the question. As if it should

have been perfectly obvious to Dad.

'For the next episode of the vlog,' said Troy impatiently. 'It's called "Don't Waste Time Getting Dressed in the Morning – Sleep in Your Uniform".'

Dad looked so impressed.

'But seriously, Dad, where are we all going to sleep?' he asked again

And that was when it dawned on me. If we were going to help Uncle Paul, the only answer to this question was . . .

My worst **NIGHTMARE**.

'You and Harper will have to share,' said Dad.

9.23 p.m.

Moving Uncle Paul in took three minutes. He didn't have any stuff.

He had his work uniform, a duvet, one change of clothes and a toe ring. That was it.

He still had the red carpet in the boot. He said he didn't want to sell that because he'd need it when he got his movie back on track again. I'm not so sure that is going to happen, but I didn't want to add to his problems by saying anything.

And now he was editing Maisie's Movie on his iPad from the comfort of his own *(my)* bedroom.

And I was trying to forget about Maisie from an inflatable mattress on the floor of our new shared room. While listening to Troy recording yet another vlog.

This episode is called *'The Six-Day Pants'.*

His **DREW DIAL RATING** is **18/10** after this one.

He has ***invented*** *(his words)* a pair of pants you can wear for **SIX STRAIGHT DAYS**. Why would anyone want that? He is now filming how to make this creation while saying, *'Guys, this is going to change the world. You'll almost never have to wash clothes again.'*

Troy doesn't wash his clothes anyway.

Making the Six-Day Pants just seems to involve cutting another leg hole in a normal pair of pants. You can *(according to Troy)* use a different combination of leg holes for three days then turn the pants inside out and do the same for the next three days.

Cutting the extra leg hole gives you four more days *(says Troy)* than your usual *'turn-your-ordinary-pants-inside-out trick'*.

GROSS.

And . . . is it just me, but . . . what on earth happens on the seventh day?

28 August

THE PREMIERE APOLOGY

Uncle Paul finished the movie and sent it to Maisie's dad in time for the premiere yesterday afternoon.

He spent hours on it. And I couldn't quite work out why he was taking so much trouble.

That was until Maisie and her dad arrived at our door.

With a box of *Krunchy Kreams*.

Maisie stood behind her dad looking very *guilty*. She definitely didn't want to catch my eye.

And then Maisie's dad just dived forward and hugged Uncle Paul. The hug was so hard and so unexpected that I saw Uncle Paul's feet lift off the ground. He even started to cough because he **couldn't breathe**.

Maisie's **dad** began to **cry**. **All over the downstairs carpet**.

This was getting seriously weird. Why were they even here?

But then it got weirder.

Maisie's dad got down on his knees. *(Which he will regret when he gets up because the downstairs carpet is still a bit damp from Uncle Paul's hotdog tears and my dad's nosebleed.)*

'Harper, I can never thank you enough. You saved Maisie's life,' he said, looking me right in the eye and clasping his hands together like he was praying very hard.

Uncle Paul winked at me.

It turns out that he had edited the movie to show Maisie *(and everyone else)* exactly what had happened with the **rogue firework**. He'd even managed a **close-up** of the sparks setting her hair on **fire**. Then he cut to me and my **quick work** with the ice bucket.

'How can we ever repay you, Harper?' Maisie's dad said, still on his knees. I wondered if he was stuck to the carpet now.

And I realised that he really meant what he was saying. He was crying tears of relief that there hadn't been a massive fire. That Maisie (and everyone else nearby) hadn't been seriously hurt.

'I'll do anything you want,' he said pleadingly.

I **wanted** to ask if he **was STUCK** to the carpet. But I resisted that temptation. And I wondered whether there **WAS** anything he could do. I had been so humiliated and embarrassed yesterday I honestly thought I would never want to see anyone from school again.

And that was when it came to me . . .

Not the idea of asking for an iPhone. I did **WANT** to ask for an iPhone and a trip to Laser Force. But I also resisted that temptation. Because there was something I wanted **much, much** more than that . . .

'Well, there is one thing that you could do,' I said.

'Tell me,' he said. 'Anything.'

'We've been raising money for a new stairlift at school. My friend Edward needs to use it, but it breaks all the time. We've raised quite a lot already, but we are still a bit short.'

'No problem,' he said. 'How much do you need?'

'£1,187.27,' I said.

That was clearly more than he had in mind. Because he jerked. Then tried to jump up off his knees. In **SHOCK**. Which confirmed that he was **definitely** a **bit stuck** to the carpet. He made it to his feet (in a move that would have been epic if he'd been lilo loafing), but there was a **CRUNCHING** sound. Which was his trousers separating from the carpet.

'How much?' he squealed. 'That is a lot more . . . errrr a little bit more . . . than I was errrr . . . but errr . . . not a problem. I'll get that arranged.'

I couldn't believe it. I wasn't sure I had ever felt quite so happy. We'd done it.

We'd got the money for the stairlift. At last.

WE DID IT. WE DID IT. WE DID IT.

As they went to leave, Maisie finally looked up.

'I'm sorry, Harper. I was really mean,' she said. **Quietly.** Hoping that no one would hear her. **BUT SHE SAID IT. SHE SAID SORRY. AND SHE ADMITTED SHE HAD BEEN MEAN.**

'And your uncle is a really good movie maker. The video footage was awesome.'

'I knew he would be,' I said. *'But you were so rude to him at the party. Saying that he wasn't a movie producer in front of everybody.'*

'I'm really sorry, Uncle Paul,' said Maisie. **Wow. Two** sorrys in **one** minute. It must be a Maisie record. And she even remembered his name this time.

The smile on Uncle Paul's face was huge. I don't think that I've seen him this pleased since he taught Leonardo DiCaprio to dance to the *Star Wars* theme tune.

'And would you like to come to a sleepover at my house tonight?' Maisie added.

But I had meant it when I said I was done trying to be part of **Team Maisie.** So I said something that I never *dreamed* I would hear myself say . . .

'Thanks, Maisie, but I'm good . . . I'm staying at Edward's tonight with Priya.'

And, for the second time in one day, I had never felt quite so happy.

1 September

ONE LAST THING

Back to school tomorrow.

And although this happens every single year, it always seems to come as a **major** shock to my mum and dad. And the evening is spent panicking about whether Troy has got the right kit to start the new term with. They never ever seem to wonder whether I have everything I need though.

Last year, I had grown out of all of my school shirts, so Dad went out and bought some **new** ones. **For Troy.** And made me wear his **old** ones. When I mentioned that the arms were way too long, he just **cut them** shorter with the **garden shears**.

This morning started off normally. And by that I mean stuff was happening that I am sure would never happen in any other family but the Drews.

Dad was practising Lilo Loafing in the paddling pool. Apparently he's sacked his coach at the local

pool and is now working on his own training programme. But Troy and Frankie still **hadn't** emptied out the bath-bomb water. Which had turned quite slimy after 13 days of being left out in the sun. My dad had been *SLIDING* all over the place and was now struggling to get up after he'd slipped into the SPLITS position on the grass.

Mum was inside teaching the Prune how to do fractions with a pile of raisins. Except that the Prune couldn't stop eating the raisins. He isn't stupid – this was a sure-fire way to end the lesson early. But he wasn't getting off that easily and even when there was only one left, Mum began dissecting the solo raisin just to keep things going.

Troy was upstairs recording a new episode of his vlog. Another cooking-based one. Called *'Who Needs a Saucepan?'* (Not Troy. I had never seen him use a saucepan. Ever.) He had taken the kettle up to our shared bedroom and was demonstrating how you could cook frankfurters in it. *'Just fill it up, boil the water, put* the frankfurters in, keep it boiling. Guys, once you master this, you'll never need to step foot in a kitchen again,' he was saying into the camera.

Uncle Paul was out. Visiting Leonardo DiCaprio.

But there has been some brilliant news for Uncle Paul. The movie he'd made for Maisie had been such a hit that Maisie's mum had shown it to all her friends. And now Uncle Paul had been **booked** to film **three weddings**, a **swimming gala**, **two bar mitzvahs**, a **morris dance** and Douglas Joiner's next **eating competition**.

I am so pleased for him. It is not **quite** Hollywood, but maybe Uncle Paul's movie career is not over just yet. And he definitely thinks this is the start of something big, because the toe ring is **back** on his finger.

Now, is it just me . . . but if you knew that someone else had been wearing that thing on their toe, would you want to wear it at all? Let alone on your hand.

Anyway, at this rate

(according to Uncle Paul), he'll be able to get Leonardo home and have Chris Hemsworth back for filming within three months. Or (if you speak to my dad about it) he'll be able to move out of our house and back to his house within three months.

Interestingly, Uncle Paul has decided that whatever happens, he is keeping his job at the supermarket. He says he loves the atmosphere. My mum says it must be 'in his genes'. I can only think that this will mean even more trips to the supermarket than we had before.

The Prune has obviously just eaten the last raisin because I can hear Mum shouting something like, 'Would you eat a calculator if I put that in front of you?' Of course he **wouldn't**. He is **not** ignorant. A calculator would be a serious advantage in this house – there is no way the Prune would try to damage it.

At the same moment, Uncle Paul arrived home.

'I've got the answer!' he shouted as he came through the door.

OMG. This could mean anything. The answer to what?

LIFE, MUM'S FRACTION QUESTIONS, WHERE TO
BUY A NEW WIG? *(Because he looked suspiciously like
he might have started adding a few extensions to his
hair in the last few days. Ever since he got the news
about filming the morris dance.)*

'To the downstairs carpet problemo,' he said. 'I
found this in the boot of the car.'

Uncle Paul **hauled** a red carpet in through the front
door. The one he had bought from OnlineCarpets for his
film premieres.

'If we cut it in half, it will fit perfectly,' he said,
clearly thinking this was a brilliant idea. 'And the best
thing about it is, you'll feel like a movie star every
time you walk out of the door.'

I think that the last bit was a bit of a stretch. But it
wasn't a bad idea and would be a big improvement on
what we currently had. And it is red. Which means that
next time my grandad's tooth or my dad's nose explodes,
you won't even see the stains.

My dad and Uncle Paul spent the rest of the afternoon

trying to fit the new carpet. But Mum had to finish it off. She decided my dad was a danger to himself after he accidentally stapled his swimming shorts to the floorboards (while still wearing them).

The doorbell went and Frankie came piling through the front door. He nearly tripped over Uncle Paul as he tried to prise the staples out of Dad's trunks.

'Sorry, Mr D. Didn't see you down there,' said Frankie. *TROYSTON. HAVE YOU SEEN THE VIEWS?'* he shouted up the stairs.

'TROYSTON' came running down the stairs with a kettle in one hand and a bag of pasta in the other hand.

'WHAT VIEWS, FRANKSTER THE PRANKSTER?' shouted Troy.

They need to work on some better nicknames for each other. Seriously.

The vlog. The cling-film one. "Who Needs a Towel?" It's gone viral. It's had 133,221 views.'

'We've made it!' screamed Troy. 'We have finally made it. I KNEW my **audience** would love this.'

My mum looked like she might burst with pride. And my dad would have got up and hugged Troy for sure. But he was still stapled to the floor.

And for once *(and just this once)*, I think I might be just a **(VERY TINY)** bit pleased for Troy. Maybe he was right. Maybe his **audience** are just like him. And maybe they do want to know the best way to put absolutely no effort into anything at all.

So who better to teach them than Troy?

While Troyston and Frankster the Prankster carried on whooping about their vlog success, my mum took the kettle off Troy to make some tea.

When she came back with the mugs for my dad and Uncle Paul, there were big hunks of **SAUSAGE** floating on the top.

But when Troy explained that he had been using the kettle to cook frankfurters, Dad said, '*Troy. That's one of the most inspirational ideas I have ever heard. And it really adds flavour to the tea.*'

Seriously? Is it just me . . . but don't people usually add *sugar* to a cup of tea? Not half a frankfurter?

Troy smiled sarcastically at me *(as if to say, 'They still like me better than you!')* and then flicked his very carefully styled hair in my face.

So . . . things are right back to normal.

And he is still **THE** most annoying person on the **planet**.

(for now).

ACKNOWLEDGEMENTS

There are a lot of people to thank for bringing the world of Harper Drew to life. But I would like to start by thanking my parents for all of the experiences I had growing up which have inspired many of the escapades in the book. While Eve and Steve Drew are not entirely based on Andy and Rita Weeks, there may be one or two similarities. I will leave you to guess which (but let's just say . . . my mum really does like bleach and maths and supermarkets). I'd also like to thank my brothers (Ciaran and Dominic) too. They are more like the Prune than Troy. Although Ciaran does spend quite a lot of time on his hair.

I'd like to thank Hilary Murray Hill at Hachette Children's Group for believing in an idea I had a long time ago that was the start of this journey. And to Debbie Foy. She let me loose on a couple of pages of a non-fiction book. She thought they were good, but if she hadn't, I suspect that I would never have been here writing this. I'd also like to tell everyone else at Hachette Children's Group how great they have been. It is a fantastic team whose enthusiasm for Harper Drew knows no bounds, and I love working with you all. Ruth Alltimes, Katy Cattell, Beth McWilliams, Hannah Bradridge, Annabel El-Kerim, Michelle Brackenborough, Nic Goode, Laura Pritchard, and of course Polly Lyall Grant, who I think really wants to go on a Drew family holiday. And to my agents at Curtis Brown, Viola Hayden and Jonny Geller. Your support and advice is always invaluable and I appreciate it very much.

Thanks to Aleksei Bitskoff for bringing the ideas in my head to life with such fantastic illustrations.

I'd also like to thank all of the people who read the earlier drafts and gave me brilliant ideas. In particular to Jane Casey whose expert advice was very gratefully received and also to Helen Pate, Lois Kent, Hannah Guthrie,

Shannon Guest, Beth Pavey, Angellica Bell, Dilys Syed and to my younger critics Florence Weeks (no relation, but great name!), Holly Townsend, Teddy Guthrie, Evie Syed and Henry Tysome.

Finally, to my family who means the world to me. My children, Evie and Teddy, you really are awesome (even when you don't listen to anything I say). And my husband Matthew. I love you all, a lot.

Kathy x

PILLGWENLLY

KATHY WEEKS

Before starting work on her children's fiction series, Kathy had quite a few jobs. She has worked on the music counter at WHSmith, been an investment banker, a waitress, a property developer, investigated missing millions for the Sultan of Brunei, founded a successful consulting business, worked for HM Treasury, and has cooked dinners at a care home for the elderly.

But her love of writing was sparked when collaborating on the bestselling children's non-fiction titles *You Are Awesome* and *Dare to Be You* with Matthew Syed. Kathy believes that all children should have confidence in their own potential and not be limited by the beliefs they (or others) hold about themselves.

Share your thoughts using #WhatsNewHarperDrew
@Kathyweeks1977 @HachetteKids